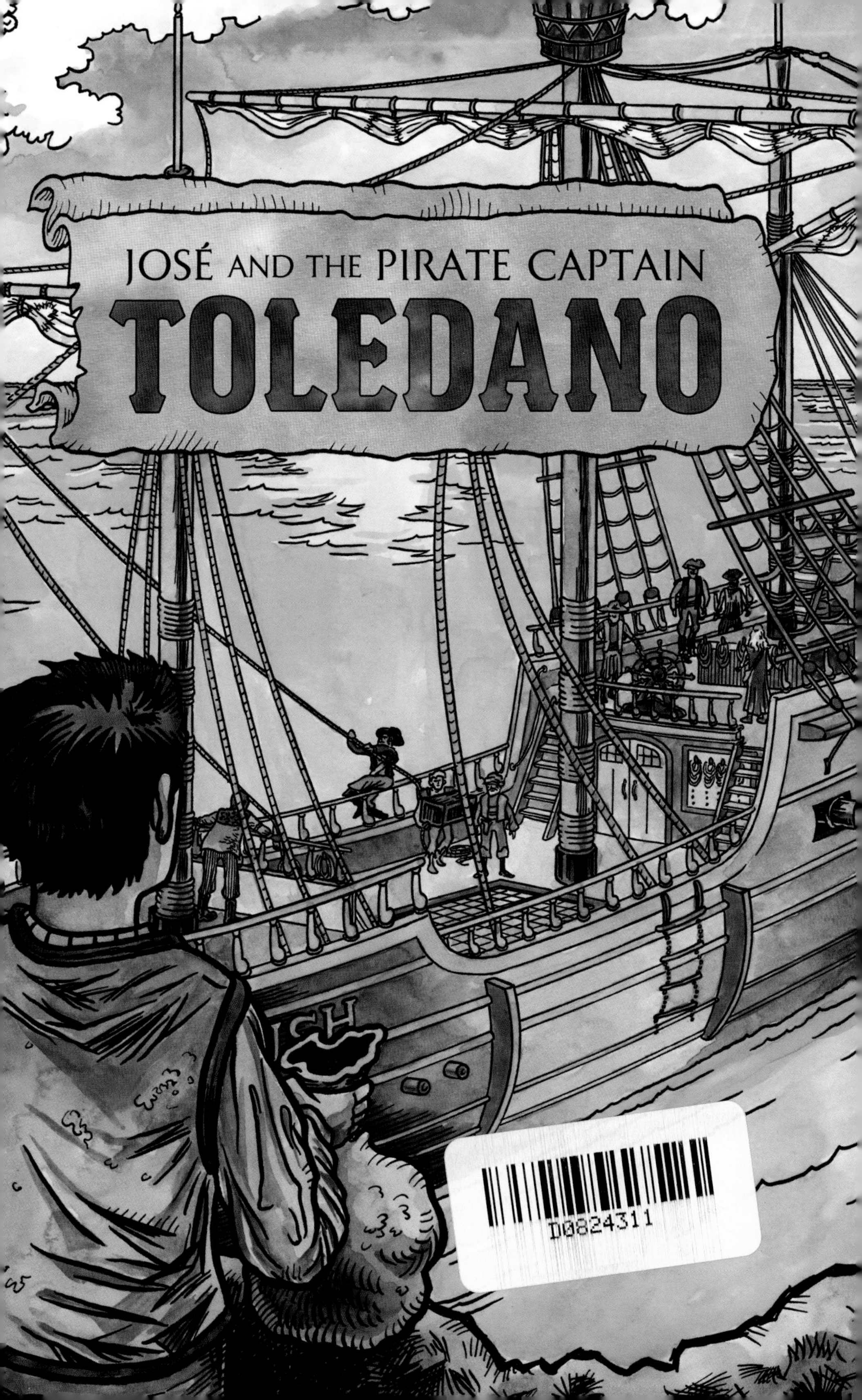
JOSÉ AND THE PIRATE CAPTAIN
TOLEDANO

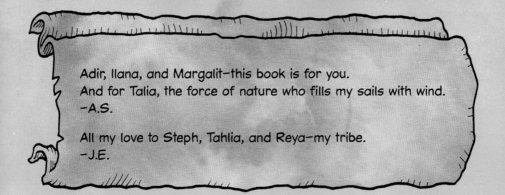

Adir, Ilana, and Margalit—this book is for you.
And for Talia, the force of nature who fills my sails with wind.
—A.S.

All my love to Steph, Tahlia, and Reya—my tribe.
—J.E.

KAR-BEN PUBLISHING®
An imprint of Lerner Publishing Group, Inc.
241 First Avenue North
Minneapolis, MN 55401 USA
Website address: www.karben.com

Main body text set in CCDaveGibbonsLower.
Typeface provided by Comicraft.

Library of Congress Cataloging-in-Publication Data

Names: Shorr, Arnon Z., author. I Edelglass, Joshua M., illustrator.
Title: Jose and the pirate captain / Arnon Z. Shorr ; illustrated by Joshua M. Edelglass.
Description: Minneapolis, MN : Kar-Ben Publishing, [2022] I Audience: Ages 8–12 I Audience: Grades
    4–6 I Summary: "Set in the shadows of the Spanish Inquisition, José and the Pirate Captain Toledano is the coming-of-age story of Jose Alfaro, who has a powerful bond with with the mysterious Pirate Captain Toledano"– Provided by publisher.
Identifiers: LCCN 2021014677 (print) I LCCN 2021014678 (ebook) I ISBN 9781728420097 (paperback) I
    ISBN 9781728446066 I ISBN 9781728444239 (ebook)
Subjects: LCSH: Graphic novels. I CYAC: Graphic novels. I Sea stories. I Pirates–Fiction. I Coming of age–
    Fiction.
Classification: LCC PZ7.7.S4736 Jo 2022 (print) I LCC PZ7.7.S4736 (ebook) I DDC 741.5/973–dc23

LC record available at https://lccn.loc.gov/2021014677
LC ebook record available at https://lccn.loc.gov/2021014678

Manufactured in the United States of America
1-49120-49289-9/7/2021

JOSÉ AND THE PIRATE CAPTAIN TOLEDANO

Arnon Z. Shorr
Joshua M. Edelglass

KAR-BEN
PUBLISHING

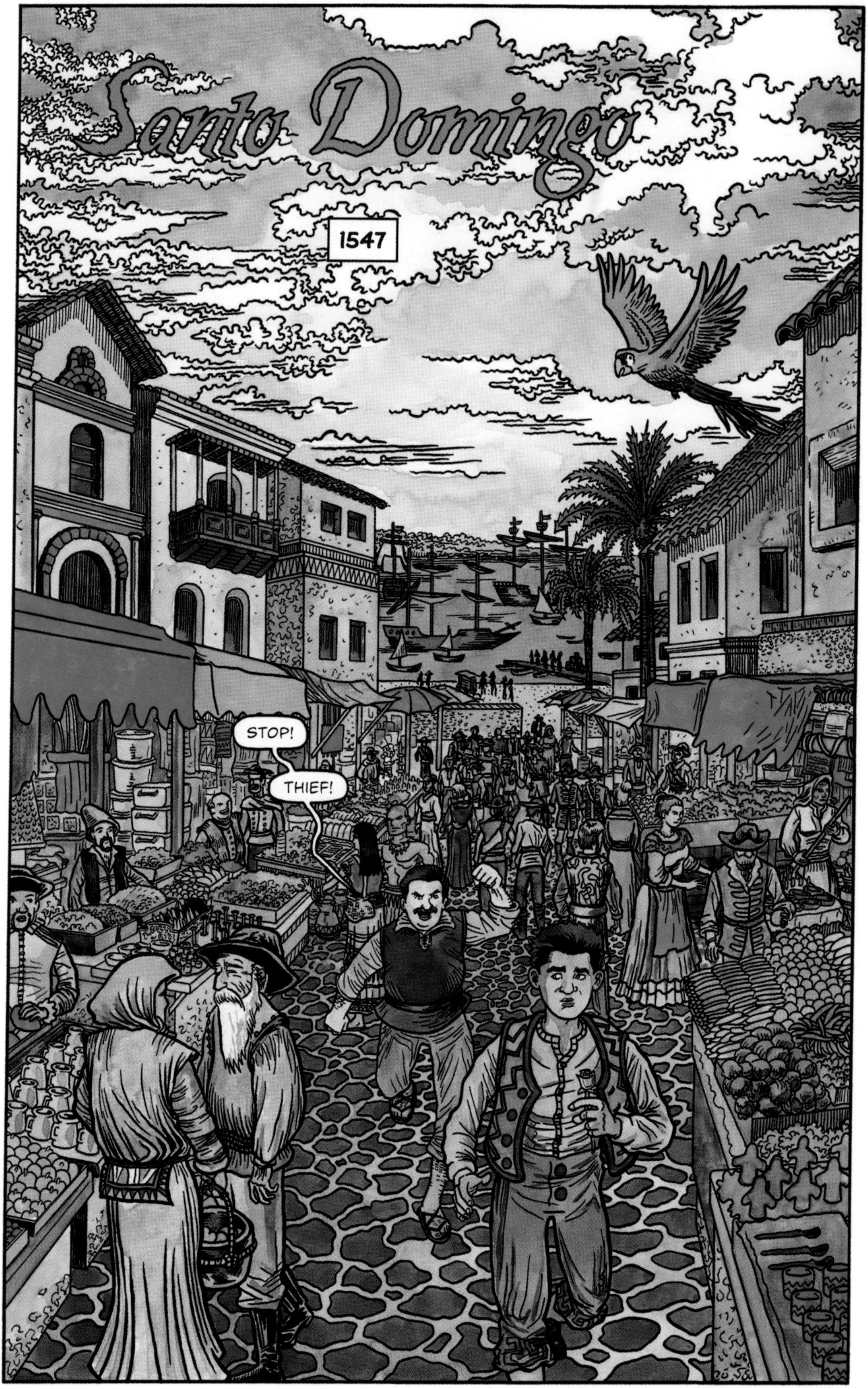
Santo Domingo
1547
STOP!
THIEF!

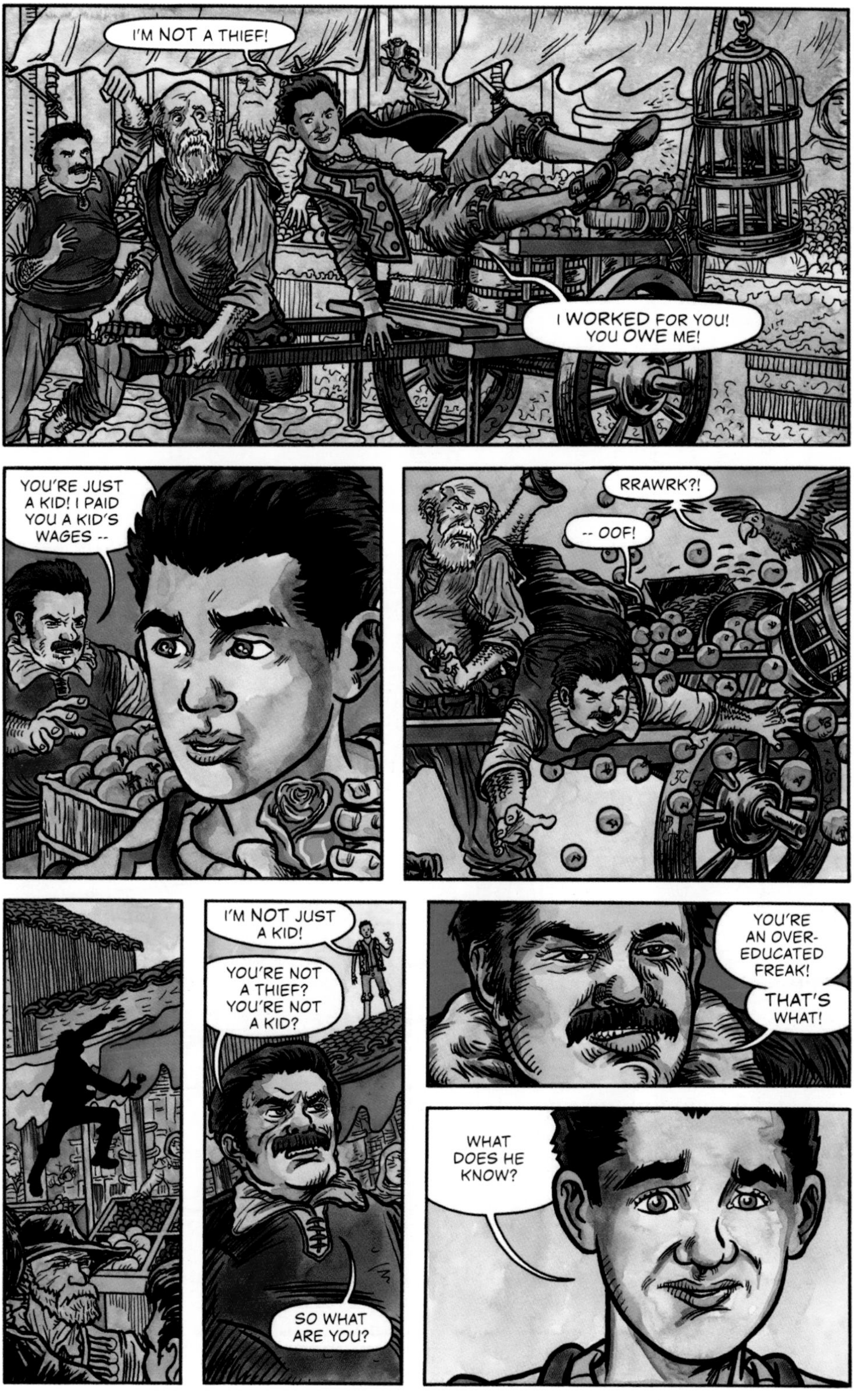
I'M NOT A THIEF!
I WORKED FOR YOU! YOU OWE ME!
YOU'RE JUST A KID! I PAID YOU A KID'S WAGES --
RRAWRK?!
-- OOF!
I'M NOT JUST A KID!
YOU'RE NOT A THIEF? YOU'RE NOT A KID?
SO WHAT ARE YOU?
YOU'RE AN OVER-EDUCATED FREAK!
THAT'S WHAT!
WHAT DOES HE KNOW?

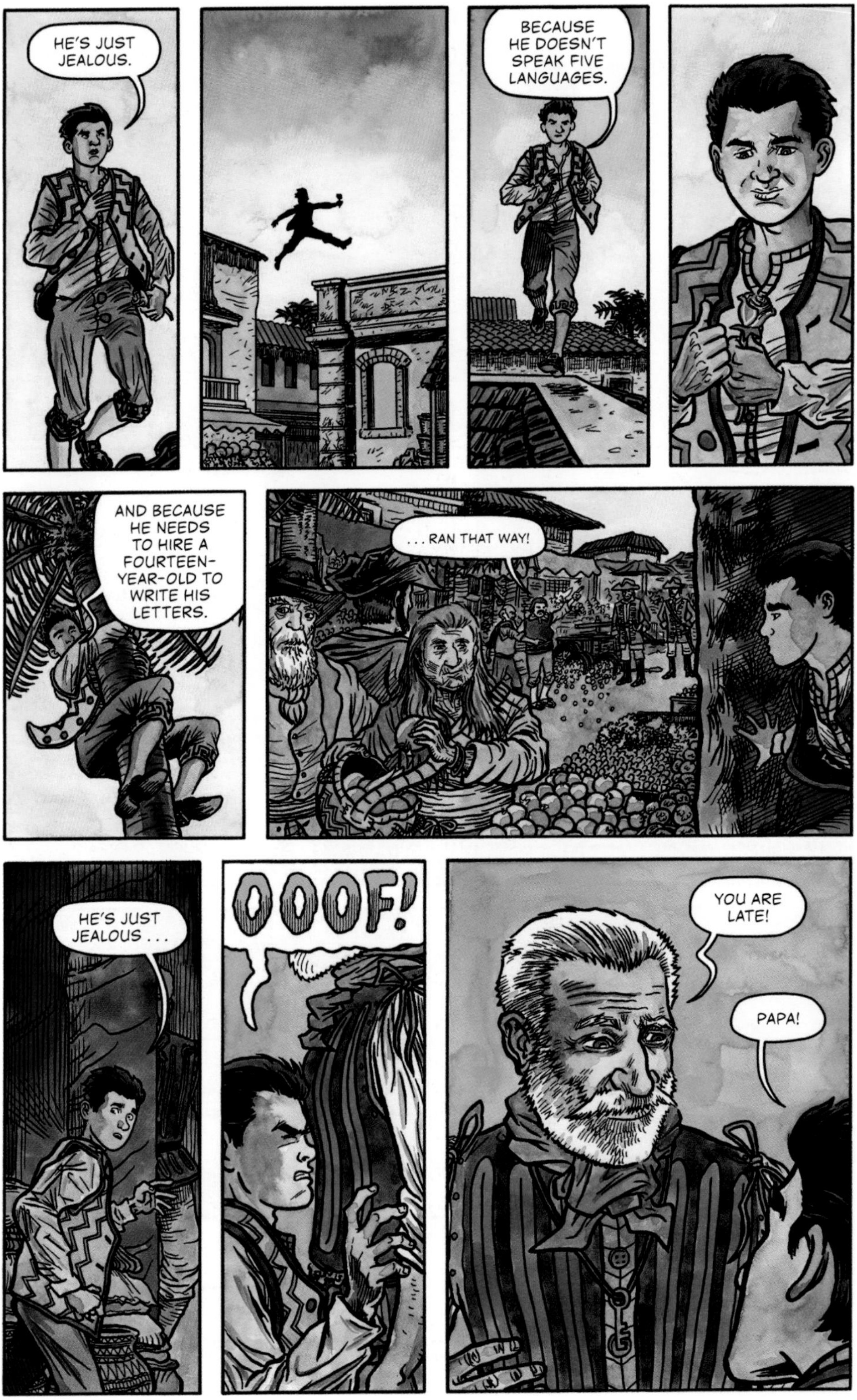
HE'S JUST JEALOUS.
BECAUSE HE DOESN'T SPEAK FIVE LANGUAGES.
AND BECAUSE HE NEEDS TO HIRE A FOURTEEN-YEAR-OLD TO WRITE HIS LETTERS.
. . . RAN THAT WAY!
HE'S JUST JEALOUS . . .
OOOF!
YOU ARE LATE!
PAPA!

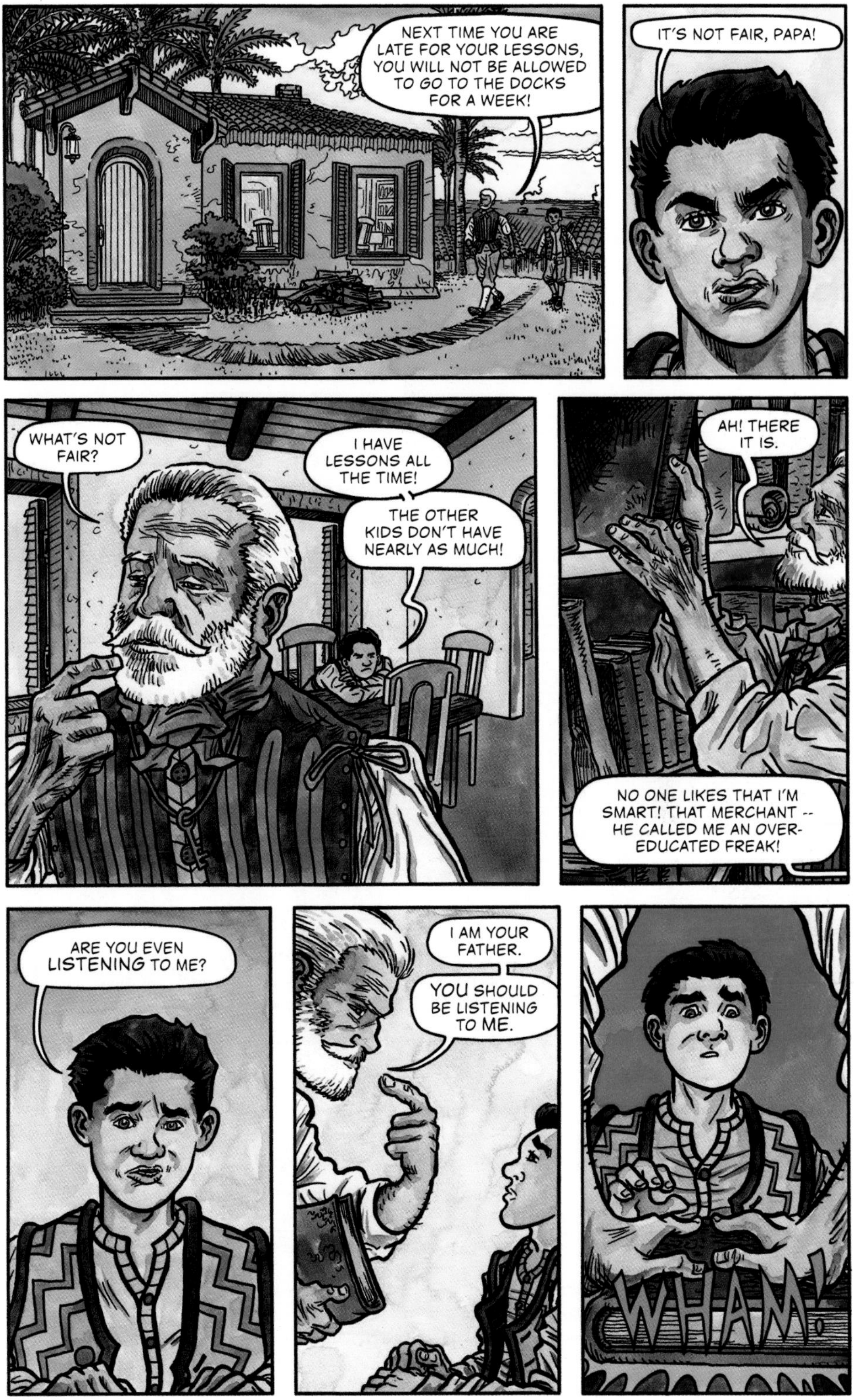
NEXT TIME YOU ARE LATE FOR YOUR LESSONS, YOU WILL NOT BE ALLOWED TO GO TO THE DOCKS FOR A WEEK!
IT'S NOT FAIR, PAPA!
WHAT'S NOT FAIR?
I HAVE LESSONS ALL THE TIME!
THE OTHER KIDS DON'T HAVE NEARLY AS MUCH!
AH! THERE IT IS.
NO ONE LIKES THAT I'M SMART! THAT MERCHANT -- HE CALLED ME AN OVER-EDUCATED FREAK!
ARE YOU EVEN LISTENING TO ME?
I AM YOUR FATHER.
YOU SHOULD BE LISTENING TO ME.
WHAM!

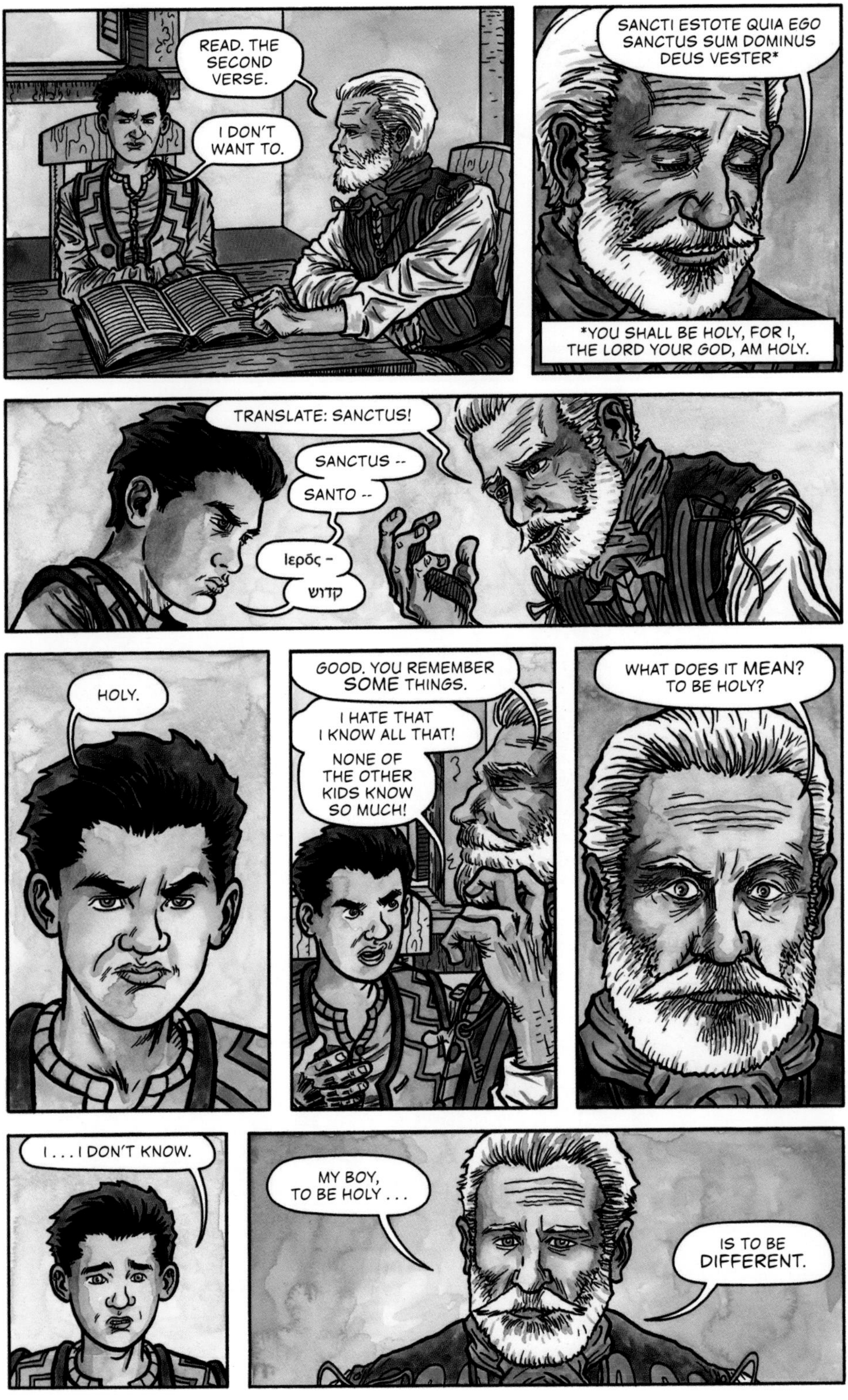
READ. THE SECOND VERSE.
I DON'T WANT TO.
SANCTI ESTOTE QUIA EGO SANCTUS SUM DOMINUS DEUS VESTER*
*YOU SHALL BE HOLY, FOR I, THE LORD YOUR GOD, AM HOLY.
TRANSLATE: SANCTUS!
SANCTUS --
SANTO --
Ιερῶς -
קדוש
HOLY.
GOOD. YOU REMEMBER SOME THINGS.
I HATE THAT I KNOW ALL THAT!
NONE OF THE OTHER KIDS KNOW SO MUCH!
WHAT DOES IT MEAN? TO BE HOLY?
I . . . I DON'T KNOW.
MY BOY, TO BE HOLY . . .
IS TO BE DIFFERENT.

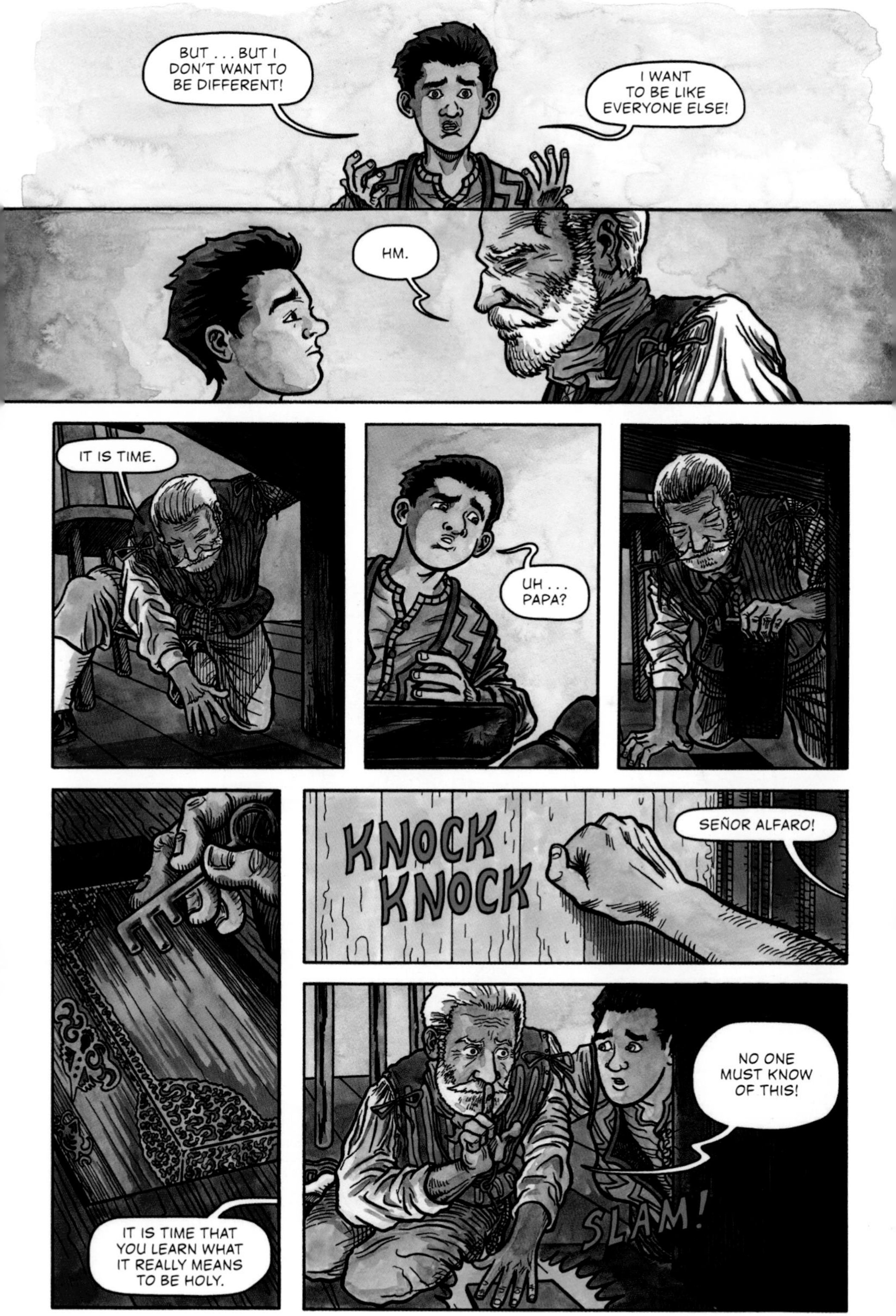
BUT . . . BUT I DON'T WANT TO BE DIFFERENT!
I WANT TO BE LIKE EVERYONE ELSE!
HM.
IT IS TIME.
UH . . . PAPA?
IT IS TIME THAT YOU LEARN WHAT IT REALLY MEANS TO BE HOLY.
KNOCK KNOCK
SEÑOR ALFARO!
NO ONE MUST KNOW OF THIS!
SLAM!

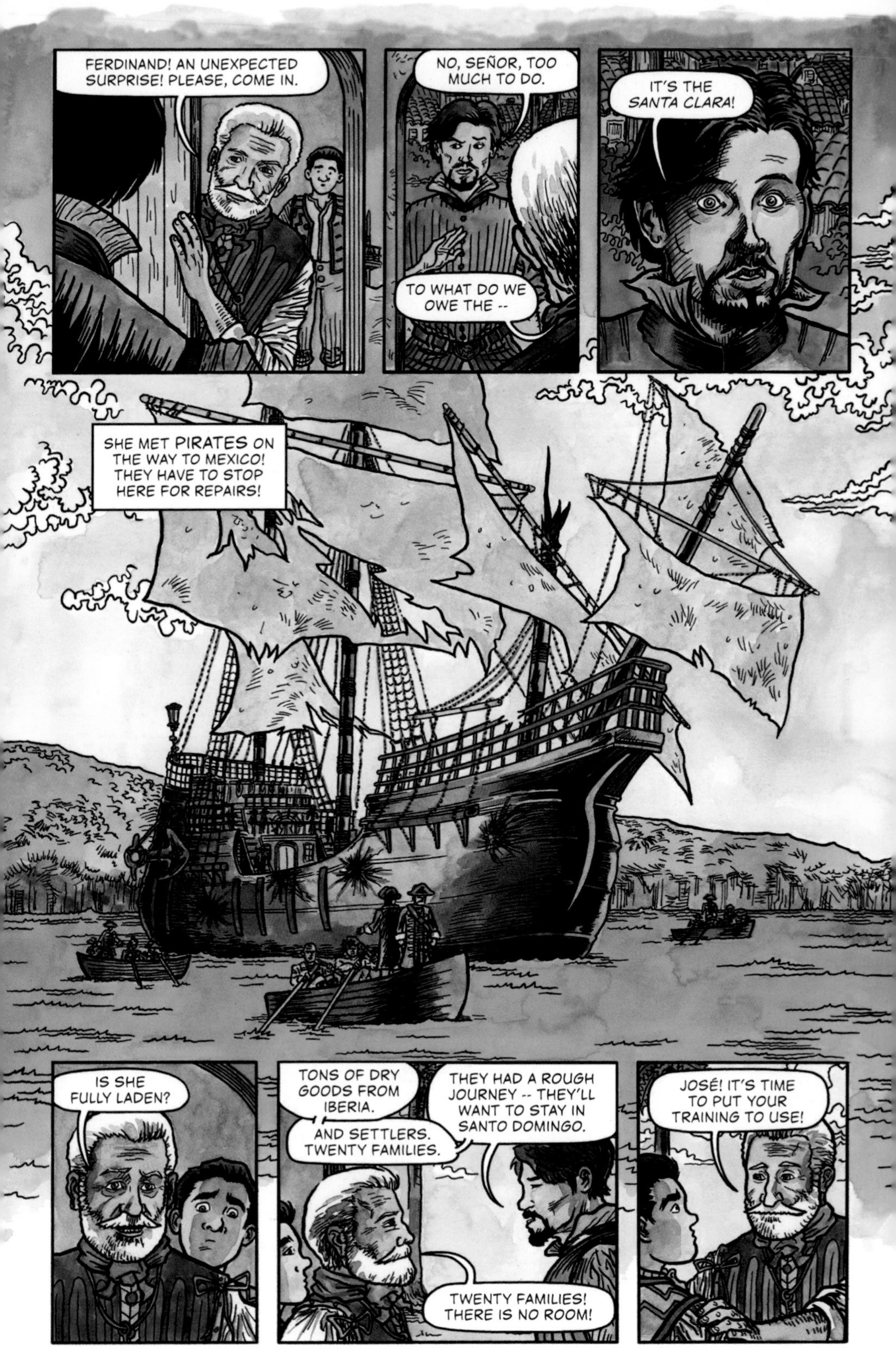
FERDINAND! AN UNEXPECTED SURPRISE! PLEASE, COME IN.
NO, SEÑOR, TOO MUCH TO DO.
TO WHAT DO WE OWE THE --
IT'S THE *SANTA CLARA*!
SHE MET PIRATES ON THE WAY TO MEXICO! THEY HAVE TO STOP HERE FOR REPAIRS!
IS SHE FULLY LADEN?
TONS OF DRY GOODS FROM IBERIA.
AND SETTLERS. TWENTY FAMILIES.
THEY HAD A ROUGH JOURNEY -- THEY'LL WANT TO STAY IN SANTO DOMINGO.
TWENTY FAMILIES! THERE IS NO ROOM!
JOSÉ! IT'S TIME TO PUT YOUR TRAINING TO USE!

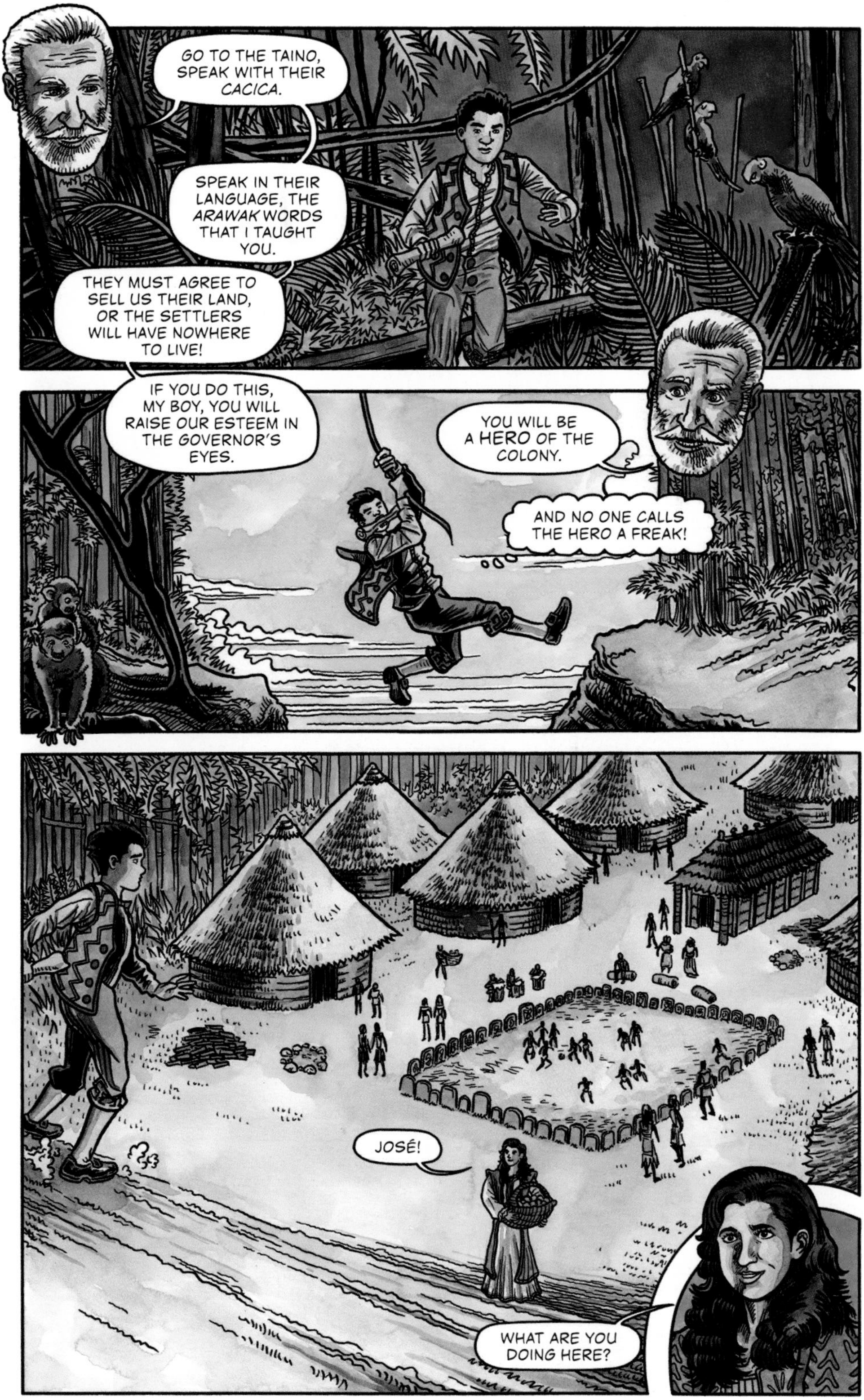
GO TO THE TAINO, SPEAK WITH THEIR *CACICA*.
SPEAK IN THEIR LANGUAGE, THE *ARAWAK* WORDS THAT I TAUGHT YOU.
THEY MUST AGREE TO SELL US THEIR LAND, OR THE SETTLERS WILL HAVE NOWHERE TO LIVE!
IF YOU DO THIS, MY BOY, YOU WILL RAISE OUR ESTEEM IN THE GOVERNOR'S EYES.
YOU WILL BE A HERO OF THE COLONY.
AND NO ONE CALLS THE HERO A FREAK!
JOSÉ!
WHAT ARE YOU DOING HERE?

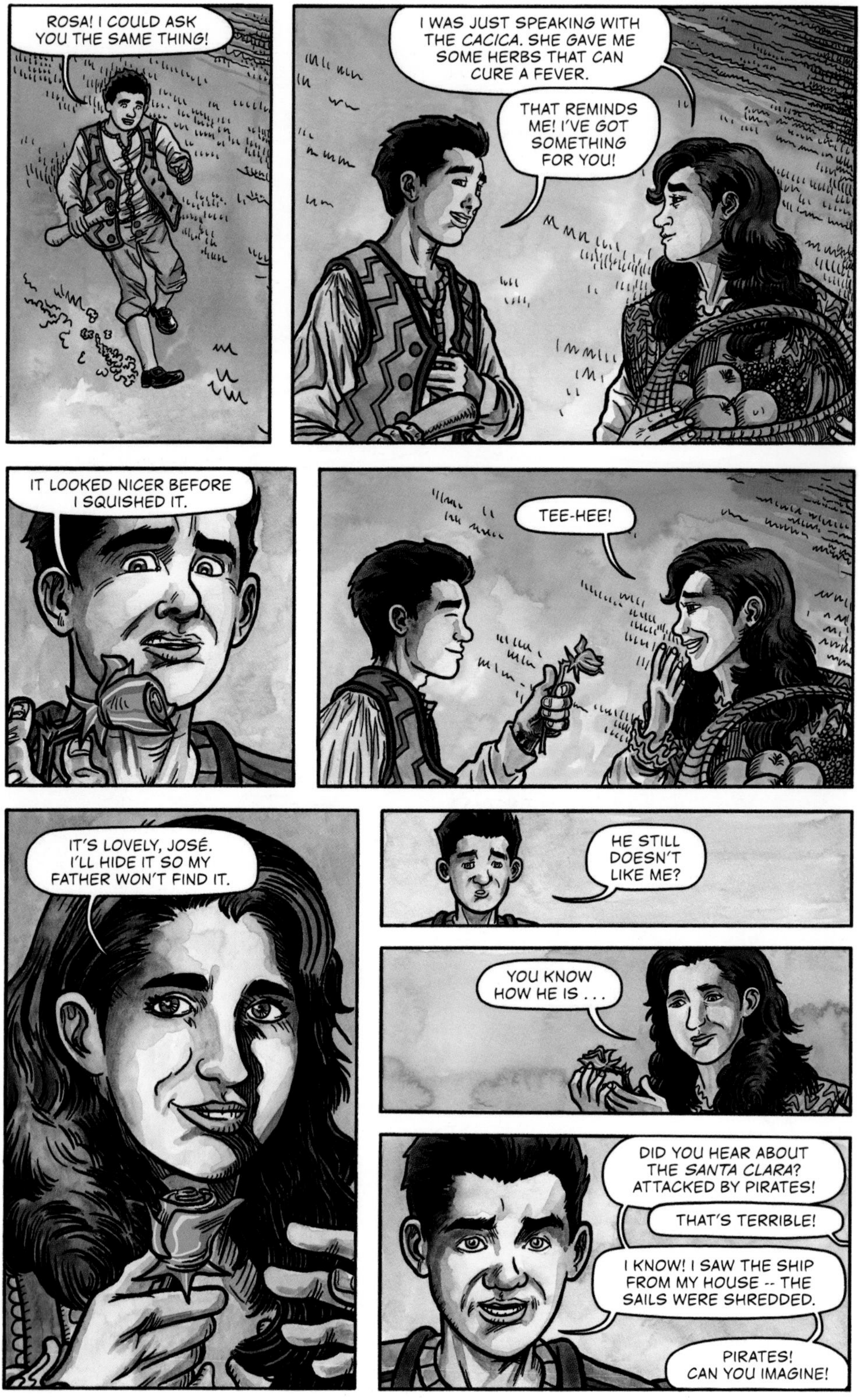
ROSA! I COULD ASK YOU THE SAME THING!
I WAS JUST SPEAKING WITH THE *CACICA*. SHE GAVE ME SOME HERBS THAT CAN CURE A FEVER.
THAT REMINDS ME! I'VE GOT SOMETHING FOR YOU!
IT LOOKED NICER BEFORE I SQUISHED IT.
TEE-HEE!
IT'S LOVELY, JOSÉ. I'LL HIDE IT SO MY FATHER WON'T FIND IT.
HE STILL DOESN'T LIKE ME?
YOU KNOW HOW HE IS . . .
DID YOU HEAR ABOUT THE *SANTA CLARA*? ATTACKED BY PIRATES!
THAT'S TERRIBLE!
I KNOW! I SAW THE SHIP FROM MY HOUSE -- THE SAILS WERE SHREDDED.
PIRATES! CAN YOU IMAGINE!

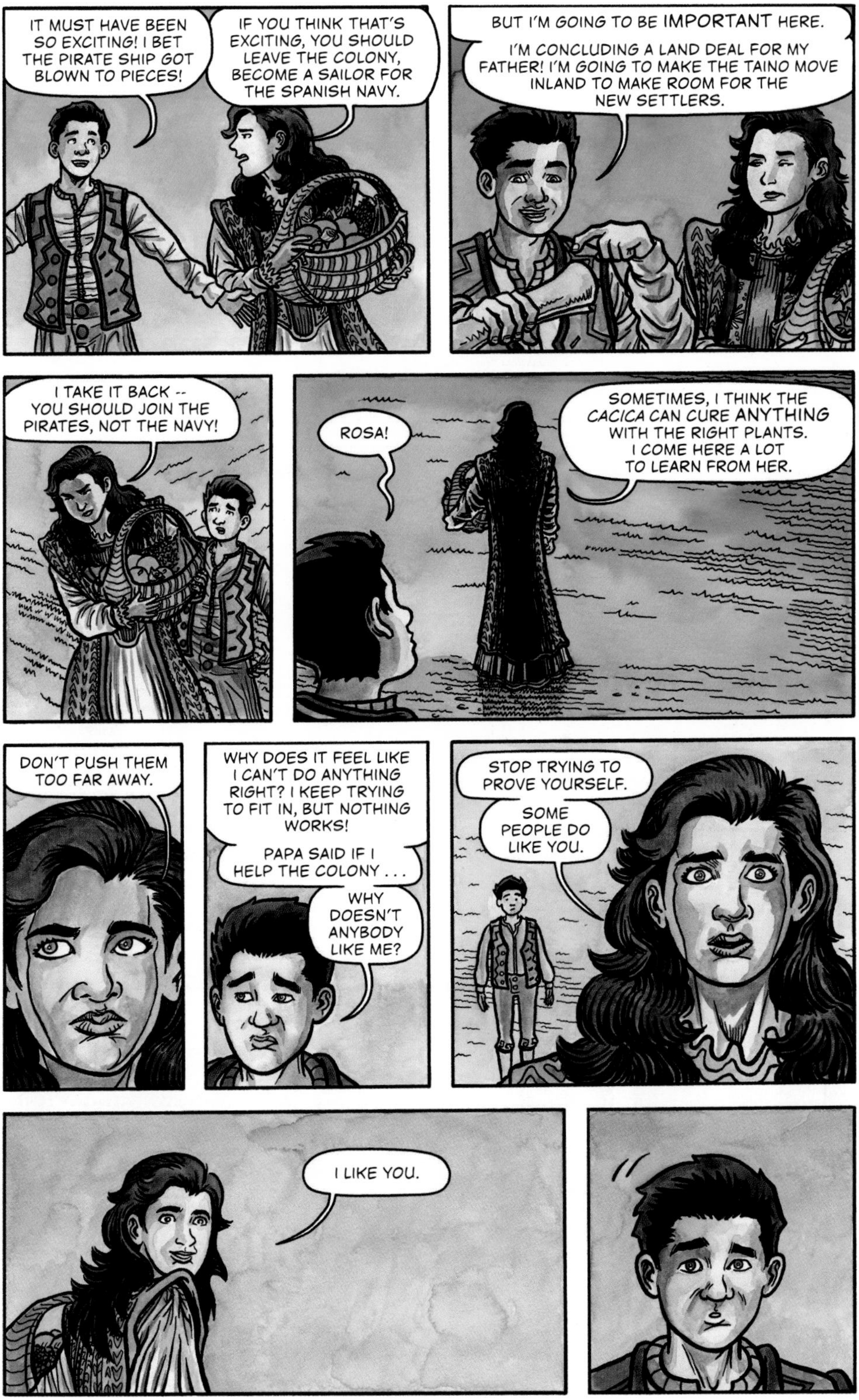
IT MUST HAVE BEEN SO EXCITING! I BET THE PIRATE SHIP GOT BLOWN TO PIECES!
IF YOU THINK THAT'S EXCITING, YOU SHOULD LEAVE THE COLONY, BECOME A SAILOR FOR THE SPANISH NAVY.
BUT I'M GOING TO BE IMPORTANT HERE.
I'M CONCLUDING A LAND DEAL FOR MY FATHER! I'M GOING TO MAKE THE TAINO MOVE INLAND TO MAKE ROOM FOR THE NEW SETTLERS.
I TAKE IT BACK -- YOU SHOULD JOIN THE PIRATES, NOT THE NAVY!
ROSA!
SOMETIMES, I THINK THE *CACICA* CAN CURE ANYTHING WITH THE RIGHT PLANTS. I COME HERE A LOT TO LEARN FROM HER.
DON'T PUSH THEM TOO FAR AWAY.
WHY DOES IT FEEL LIKE I CAN'T DO ANYTHING RIGHT? I KEEP TRYING TO FIT IN, BUT NOTHING WORKS!
PAPA SAID IF I HELP THE COLONY . . .
WHY DOESN'T ANYBODY LIKE ME?
STOP TRYING TO PROVE YOURSELF.
SOME PEOPLE DO LIKE YOU.
I LIKE YOU.

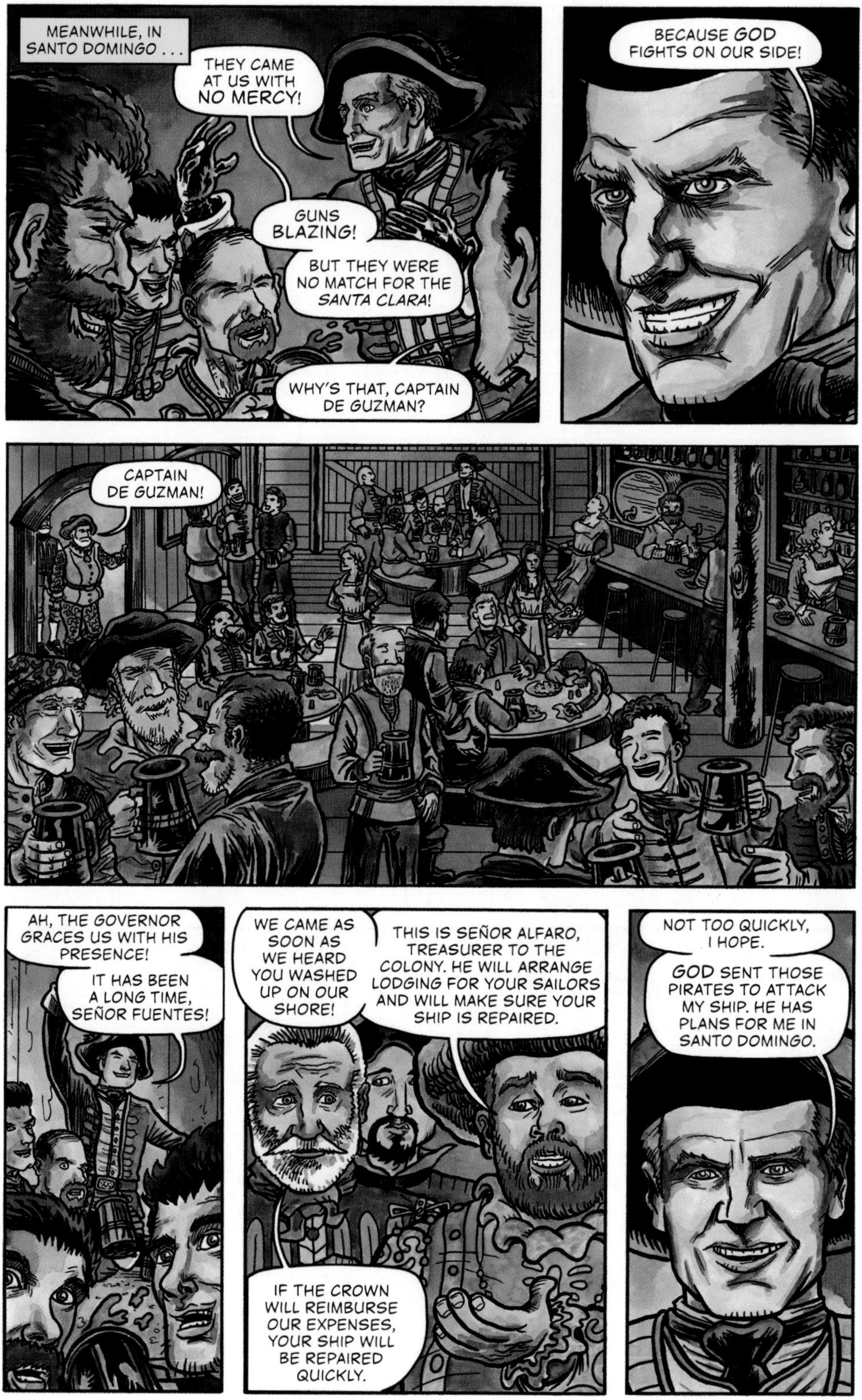
MEANWHILE, IN SANTO DOMINGO . . .
THEY CAME AT US WITH NO MERCY!
GUNS BLAZING!
BUT THEY WERE NO MATCH FOR THE SANTA CLARA!
WHY'S THAT, CAPTAIN DE GUZMAN?
BECAUSE GOD FIGHTS ON OUR SIDE!
CAPTAIN DE GUZMAN!
AH, THE GOVERNOR GRACES US WITH HIS PRESENCE!
IT HAS BEEN A LONG TIME, SEÑOR FUENTES!
WE CAME AS SOON AS WE HEARD YOU WASHED UP ON OUR SHORE!
THIS IS SEÑOR ALFARO, TREASURER TO THE COLONY. HE WILL ARRANGE LODGING FOR YOUR SAILORS AND WILL MAKE SURE YOUR SHIP IS REPAIRED.
IF THE CROWN WILL REIMBURSE OUR EXPENSES, YOUR SHIP WILL BE REPAIRED QUICKLY.
NOT TOO QUICKLY, I HOPE.
GOD SENT THOSE PIRATES TO ATTACK MY SHIP. HE HAS PLANS FOR ME IN SANTO DOMINGO.

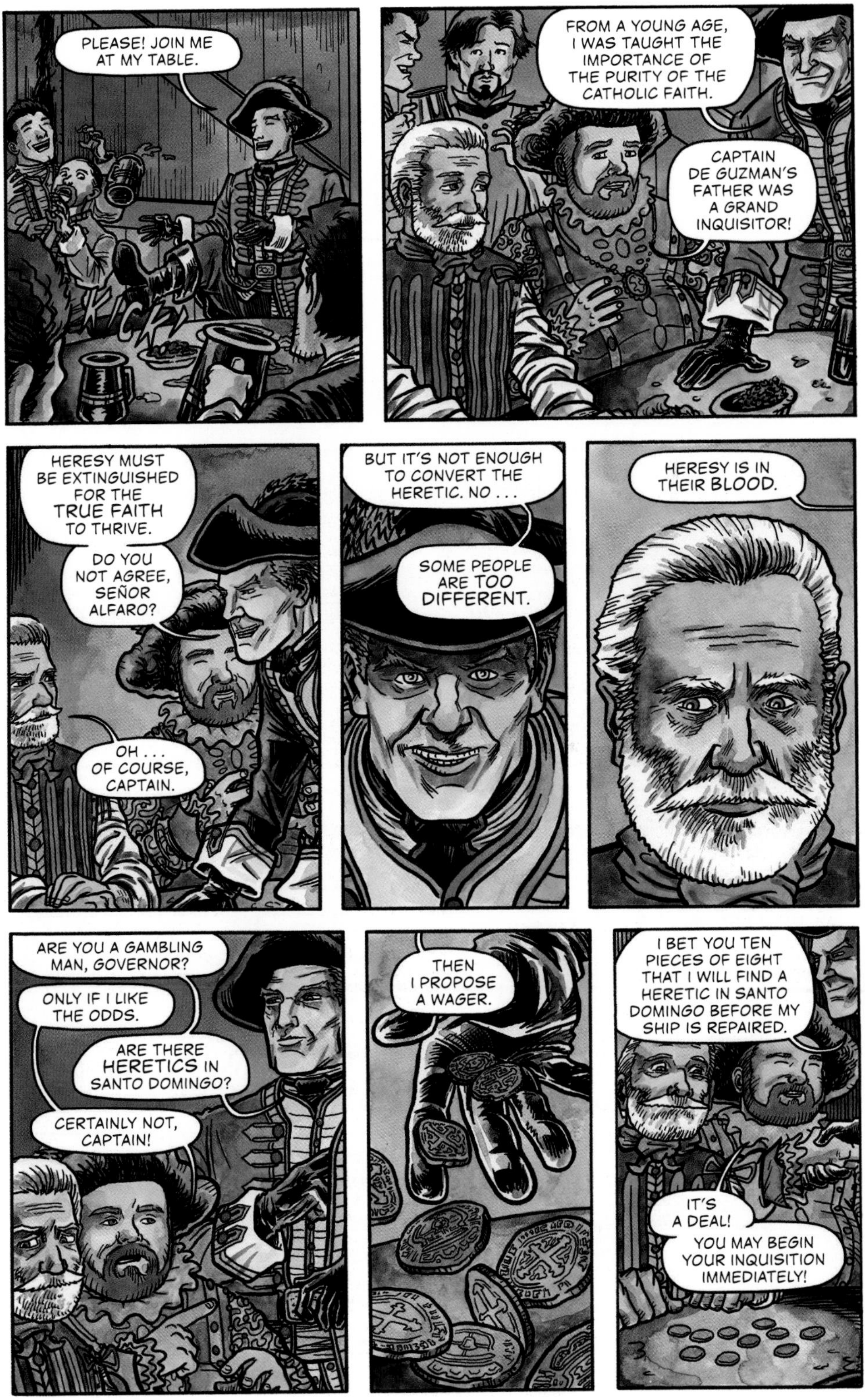
PLEASE! JOIN ME AT MY TABLE.
KICK!
FROM A YOUNG AGE, I WAS TAUGHT THE IMPORTANCE OF THE PURITY OF THE CATHOLIC FAITH.
CAPTAIN DE GUZMAN'S FATHER WAS A GRAND INQUISITOR!
HERESY MUST BE EXTINGUISHED FOR THE TRUE FAITH TO THRIVE.
DO YOU NOT AGREE, SEÑOR ALFARO?
OH . . . OF COURSE, CAPTAIN.
BUT IT'S NOT ENOUGH TO CONVERT THE HERETIC. NO . . .
SOME PEOPLE ARE TOO DIFFERENT.
HERESY IS IN THEIR BLOOD.
ARE YOU A GAMBLING MAN, GOVERNOR?
ONLY IF I LIKE THE ODDS.
ARE THERE HERETICS IN SANTO DOMINGO?
CERTAINLY NOT, CAPTAIN!
THEN I PROPOSE A WAGER.
I BET YOU TEN PIECES OF EIGHT THAT I WILL FIND A HERETIC IN SANTO DOMINGO BEFORE MY SHIP IS REPAIRED.
IT'S A DEAL!
YOU MAY BEGIN YOUR INQUISITION IMMEDIATELY!

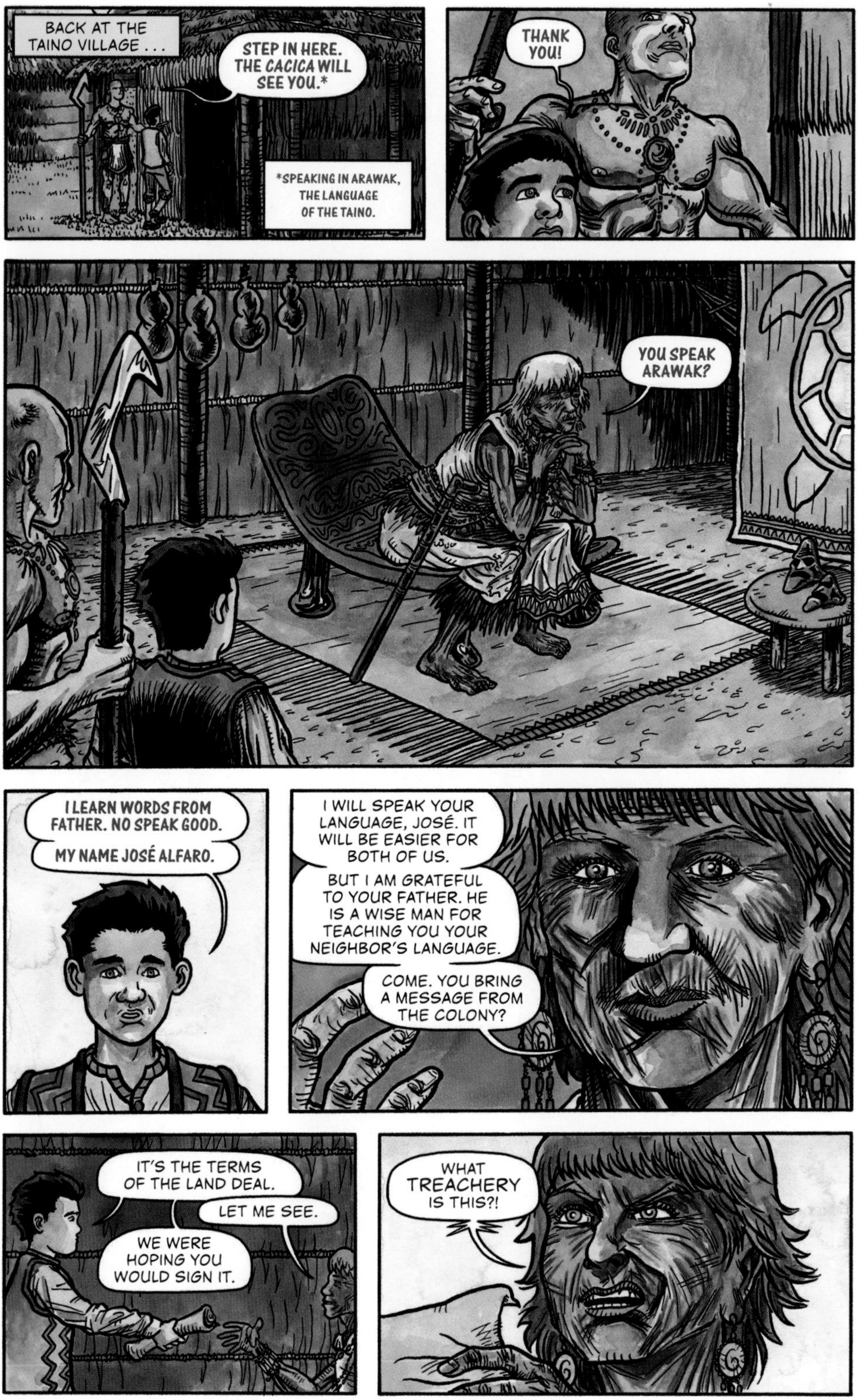
BACK AT THE TAINO VILLAGE . . .
STEP IN HERE. THE *CACICA* WILL SEE YOU.*
*SPEAKING IN ARAWAK, THE LANGUAGE OF THE TAINO.
THANK YOU!
YOU SPEAK ARAWAK?
I LEARN WORDS FROM FATHER. NO SPEAK GOOD.
MY NAME JOSÉ ALFARO.
I WILL SPEAK YOUR LANGUAGE, JOSÉ. IT WILL BE EASIER FOR BOTH OF US.
BUT I AM GRATEFUL TO YOUR FATHER. HE IS A WISE MAN FOR TEACHING YOU YOUR NEIGHBOR'S LANGUAGE.
COME. YOU BRING A MESSAGE FROM THE COLONY?
IT'S THE TERMS OF THE LAND DEAL.
LET ME SEE.
WE WERE HOPING YOU WOULD SIGN IT.
WHAT TREACHERY IS THIS?!

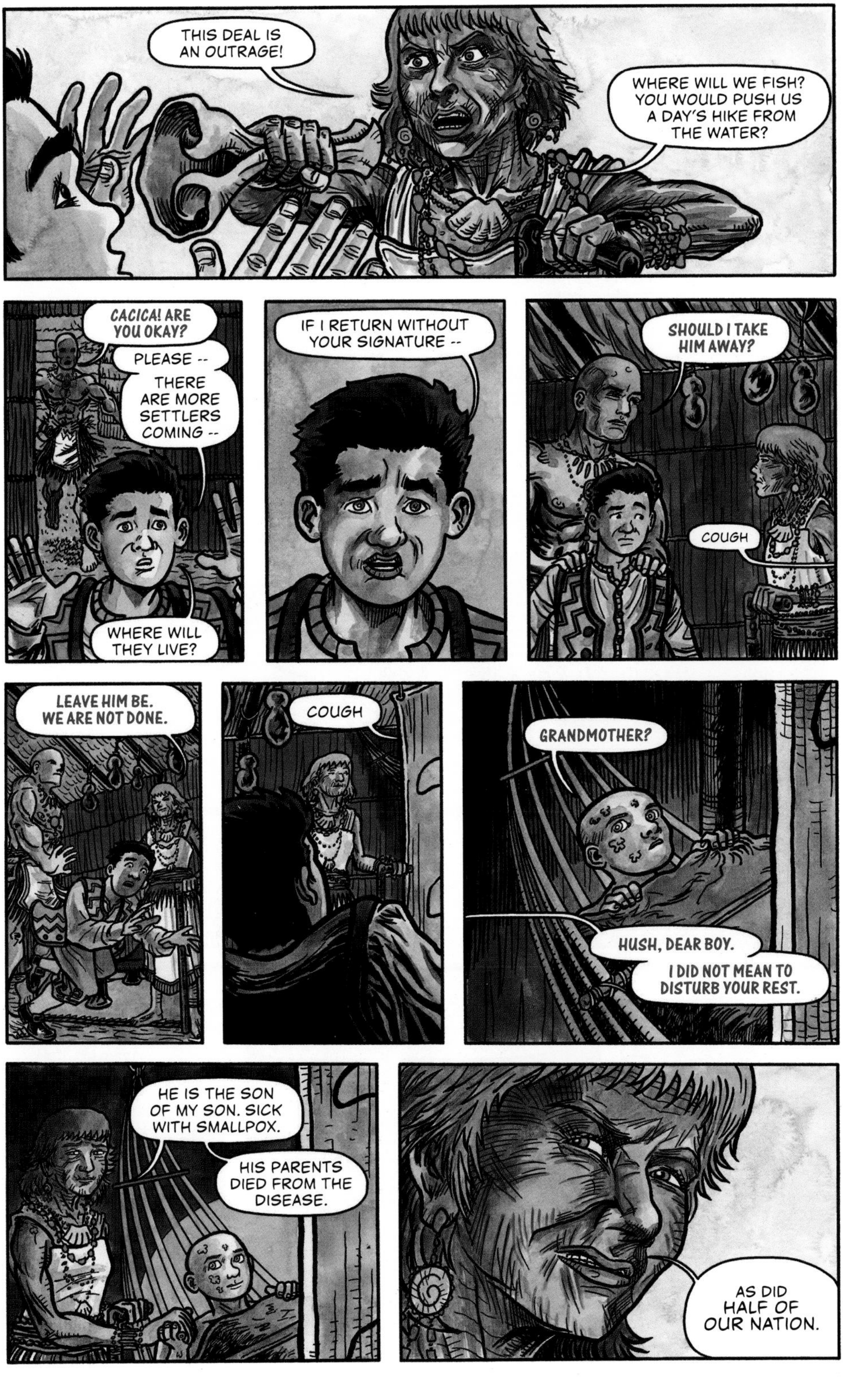

THIS DEAL IS AN OUTRAGE!
WHERE WILL WE FISH? YOU WOULD PUSH US A DAY'S HIKE FROM THE WATER?
CACICA! ARE YOU OKAY?
PLEASE --
THERE ARE MORE SETTLERS COMING --
WHERE WILL THEY LIVE?
IF I RETURN WITHOUT YOUR SIGNATURE --
SHOULD I TAKE HIM AWAY?
COUGH
LEAVE HIM BE. WE ARE NOT DONE.
COUGH
GRANDMOTHER?
HUSH, DEAR BOY.
I DID NOT MEAN TO DISTURB YOUR REST.
HE IS THE SON OF MY SON. SICK WITH SMALLPOX.
HIS PARENTS DIED FROM THE DISEASE.
AS DID HALF OF OUR NATION.

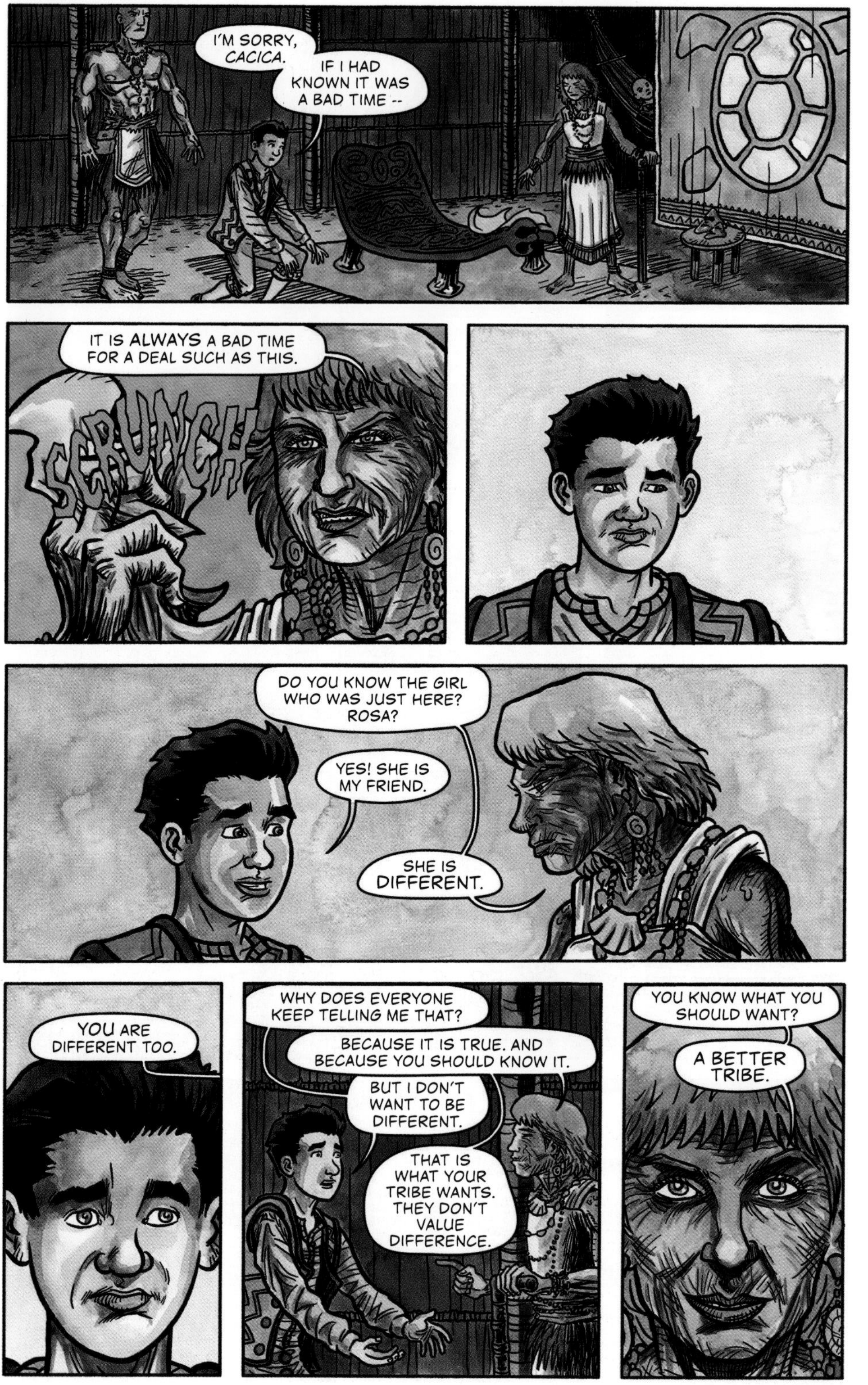
I'M SORRY, CACICA.
IF I HAD KNOWN IT WAS A BAD TIME --
IT IS ALWAYS A BAD TIME FOR A DEAL SUCH AS THIS.
SCRUNCH
DO YOU KNOW THE GIRL WHO WAS JUST HERE? ROSA?
YES! SHE IS MY FRIEND.
SHE IS DIFFERENT.
YOU ARE DIFFERENT TOO.
WHY DOES EVERYONE KEEP TELLING ME THAT?
BECAUSE IT IS TRUE. AND BECAUSE YOU SHOULD KNOW IT.
BUT I DON'T WANT TO BE DIFFERENT.
THAT IS WHAT YOUR TRIBE WANTS. THEY DON'T VALUE DIFFERENCE.
YOU KNOW WHAT YOU SHOULD WANT?
A BETTER TRIBE.

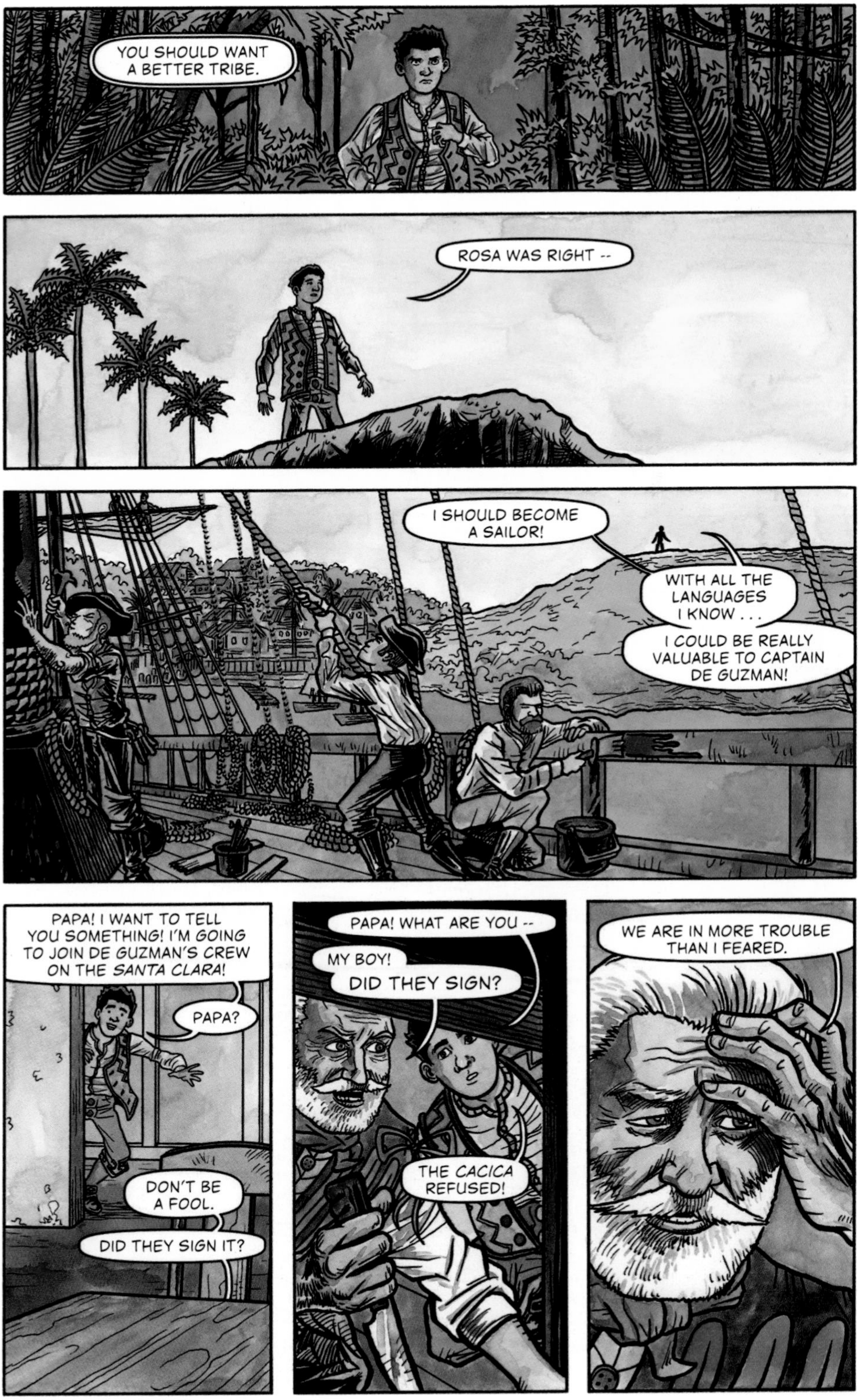
YOU SHOULD WANT A BETTER TRIBE.
ROSA WAS RIGHT --
I SHOULD BECOME A SAILOR!
WITH ALL THE LANGUAGES I KNOW . . .
I COULD BE REALLY VALUABLE TO CAPTAIN DE GUZMAN!
PAPA! I WANT TO TELL YOU SOMETHING! I'M GOING TO JOIN DE GUZMAN'S CREW ON THE *SANTA CLARA*!
PAPA?
DON'T BE A FOOL.
DID THEY SIGN IT?
PAPA! WHAT ARE YOU --
MY BOY!
DID THEY SIGN?
THE *CACICA* REFUSED!
WE ARE IN MORE TROUBLE THAN I FEARED.

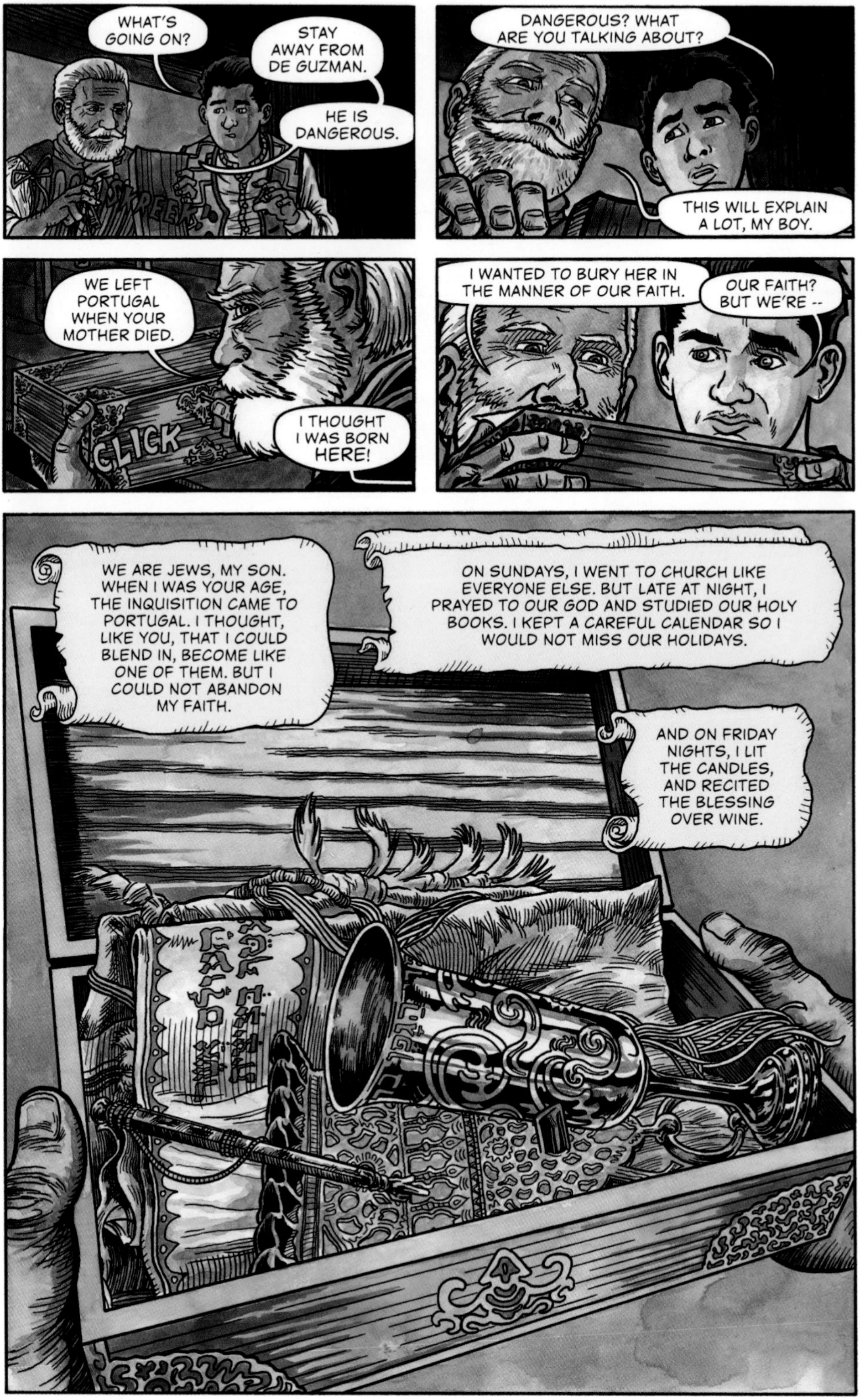
WHAT'S GOING ON?
STAY AWAY FROM DE GUZMAN.
HE IS DANGEROUS.
DANGEROUS? WHAT ARE YOU TALKING ABOUT?
THIS WILL EXPLAIN A LOT, MY BOY.
WE LEFT PORTUGAL WHEN YOUR MOTHER DIED.
CLICK
I THOUGHT I WAS BORN HERE!
I WANTED TO BURY HER IN THE MANNER OF OUR FAITH.
OUR FAITH? BUT WE'RE --
WE ARE JEWS, MY SON. WHEN I WAS YOUR AGE, THE INQUISITION CAME TO PORTUGAL. I THOUGHT, LIKE YOU, THAT I COULD BLEND IN, BECOME LIKE ONE OF THEM. BUT I COULD NOT ABANDON MY FAITH.
ON SUNDAYS, I WENT TO CHURCH LIKE EVERYONE ELSE. BUT LATE AT NIGHT, I PRAYED TO OUR GOD AND STUDIED OUR HOLY BOOKS. I KEPT A CAREFUL CALENDAR SO I WOULD NOT MISS OUR HOLIDAYS.
AND ON FRIDAY NIGHTS, I LIT THE CANDLES, AND RECITED THE BLESSING OVER WINE.

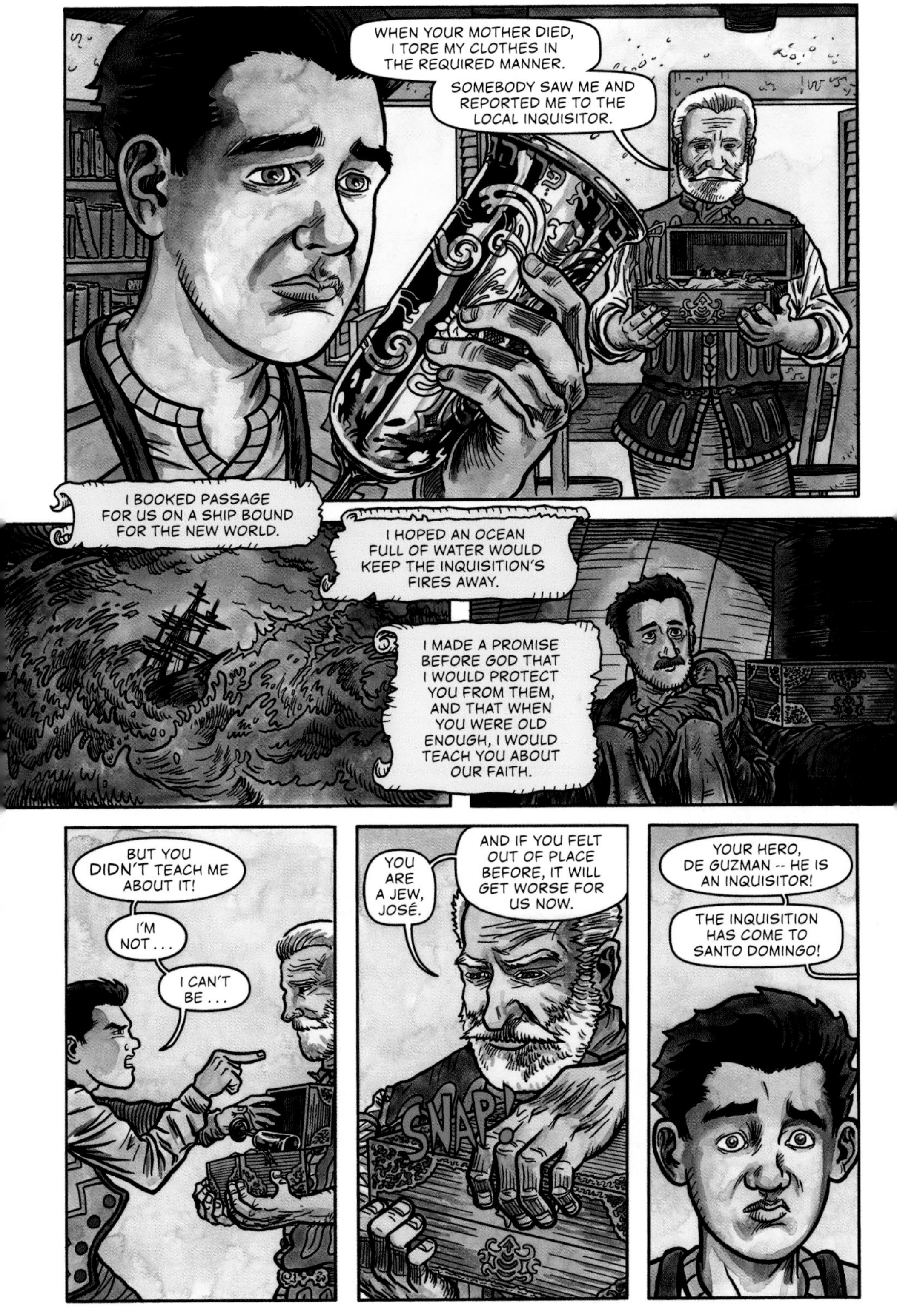
WHEN YOUR MOTHER DIED, I TORE MY CLOTHES IN THE REQUIRED MANNER.
SOMEBODY SAW ME AND REPORTED ME TO THE LOCAL INQUISITOR.
I BOOKED PASSAGE FOR US ON A SHIP BOUND FOR THE NEW WORLD.
I HOPED AN OCEAN FULL OF WATER WOULD KEEP THE INQUISITION'S FIRES AWAY.
I MADE A PROMISE BEFORE GOD THAT I WOULD PROTECT YOU FROM THEM, AND THAT WHEN YOU WERE OLD ENOUGH, I WOULD TEACH YOU ABOUT OUR FAITH.
BUT YOU DIDN'T TEACH ME ABOUT IT!
I'M NOT . . .
I CAN'T BE . . .
YOU ARE A JEW, JOSÉ.
AND IF YOU FELT OUT OF PLACE BEFORE, IT WILL GET WORSE FOR US NOW.
SNAP!
YOUR HERO, DE GUZMAN -- HE IS AN INQUISITOR!
THE INQUISITION HAS COME TO SANTO DOMINGO!

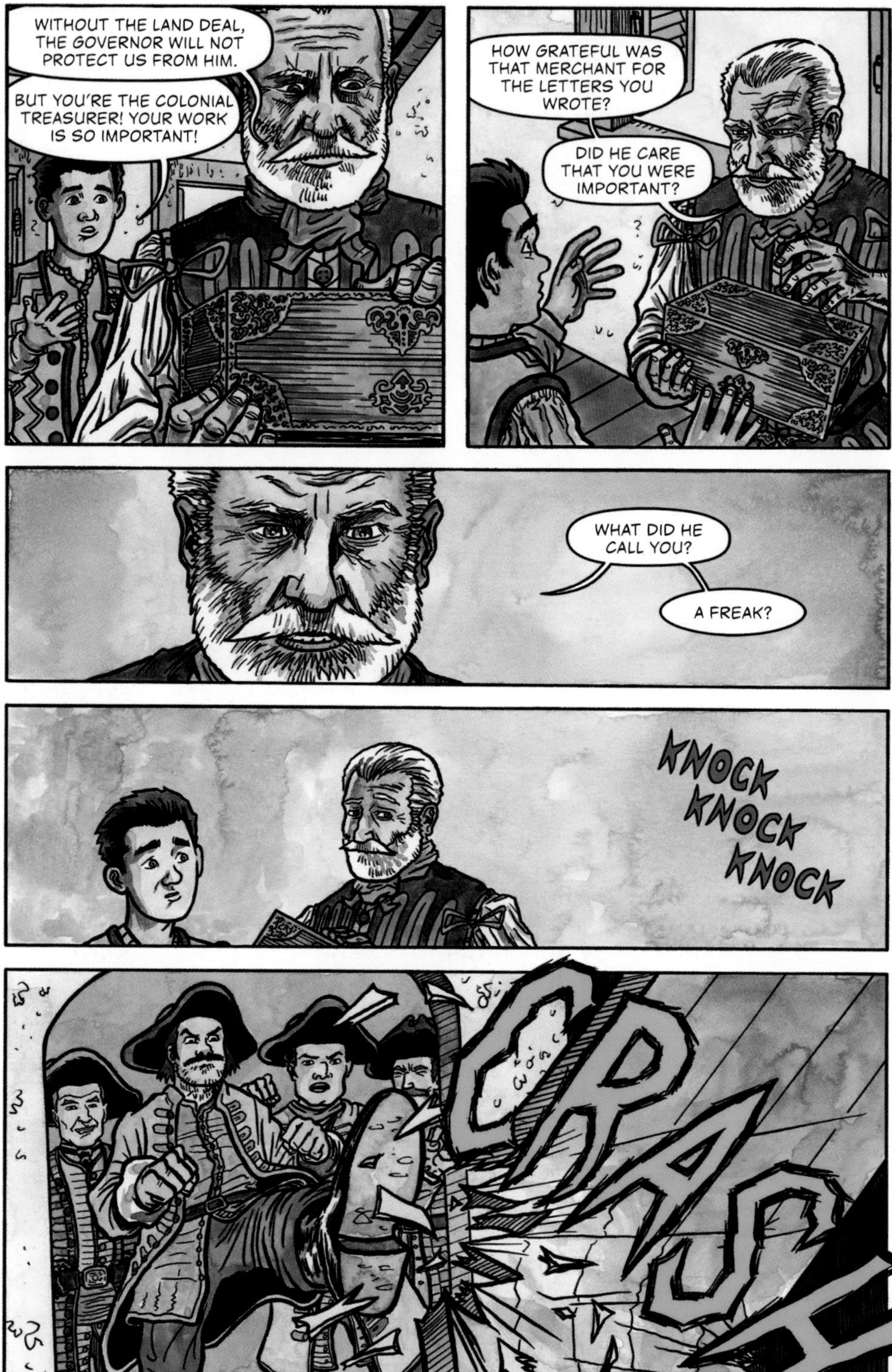
WITHOUT THE LAND DEAL, THE GOVERNOR WILL NOT PROTECT US FROM HIM.
BUT YOU'RE THE COLONIAL TREASURER! YOUR WORK IS SO IMPORTANT!
HOW GRATEFUL WAS THAT MERCHANT FOR THE LETTERS YOU WROTE?
DID HE CARE THAT YOU WERE IMPORTANT?
WHAT DID HE CALL YOU?
A FREAK?
KNOCK KNOCK KNOCK
CRASH!

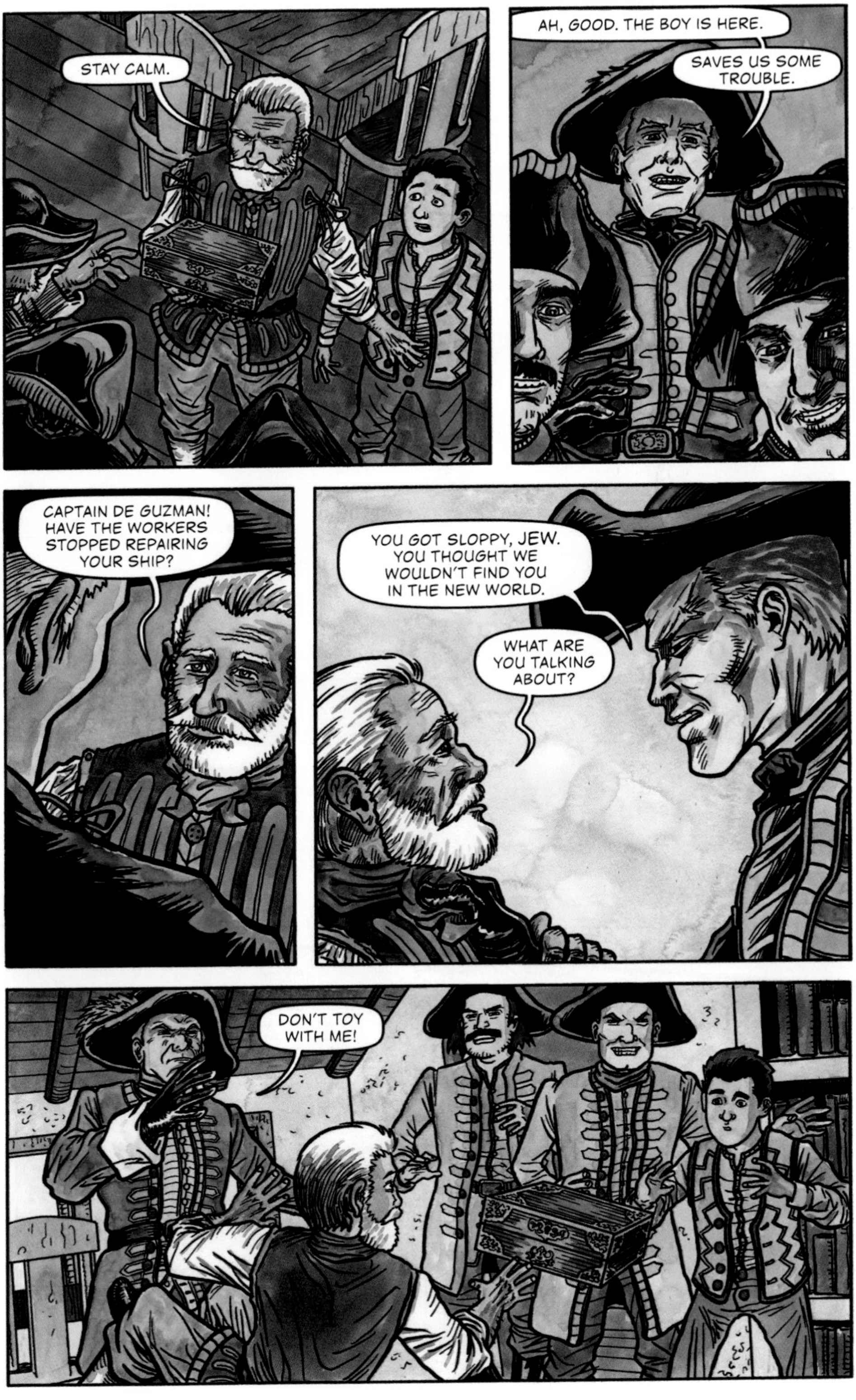
STAY CALM.
AH, GOOD. THE BOY IS HERE.
SAVES US SOME TROUBLE.
CAPTAIN DE GUZMAN! HAVE THE WORKERS STOPPED REPAIRING YOUR SHIP?
YOU GOT SLOPPY, JEW. YOU THOUGHT WE WOULDN'T FIND YOU IN THE NEW WORLD.
WHAT ARE YOU TALKING ABOUT?
DON'T TOY WITH ME!

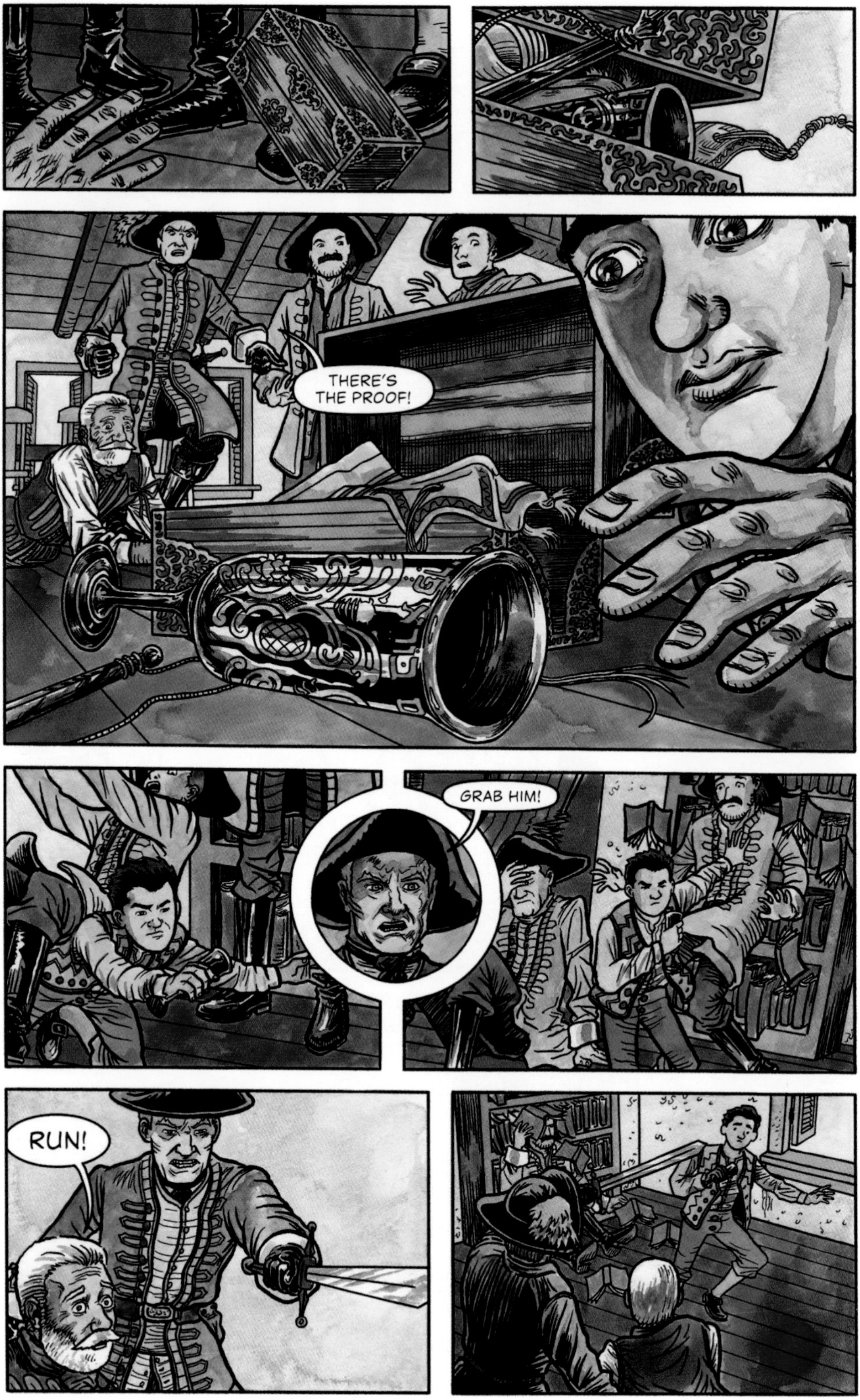
THERE'S THE PROOF!
GRAB HIM!
RUN!

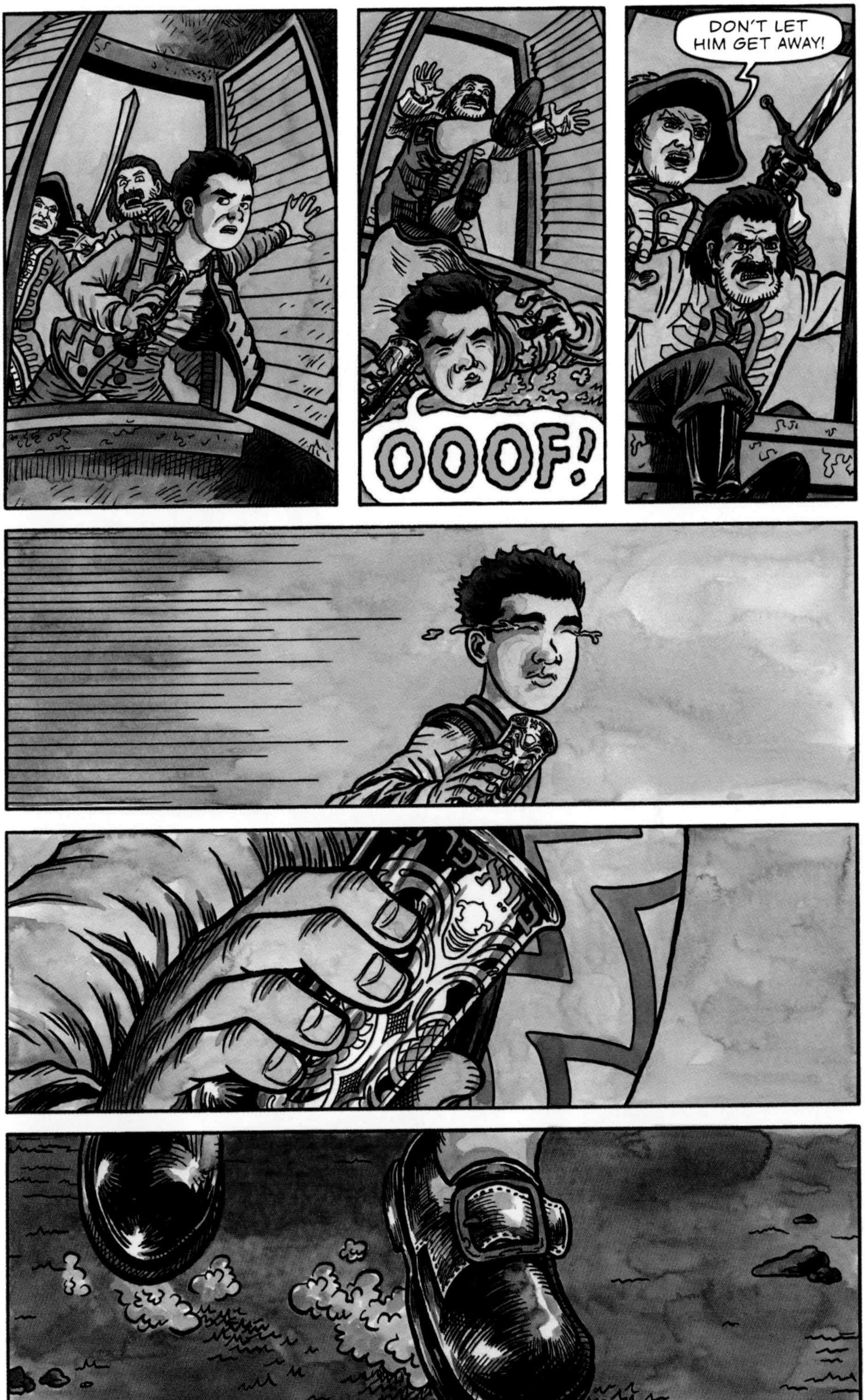
OOOF!
DON'T LET HIM GET AWAY!

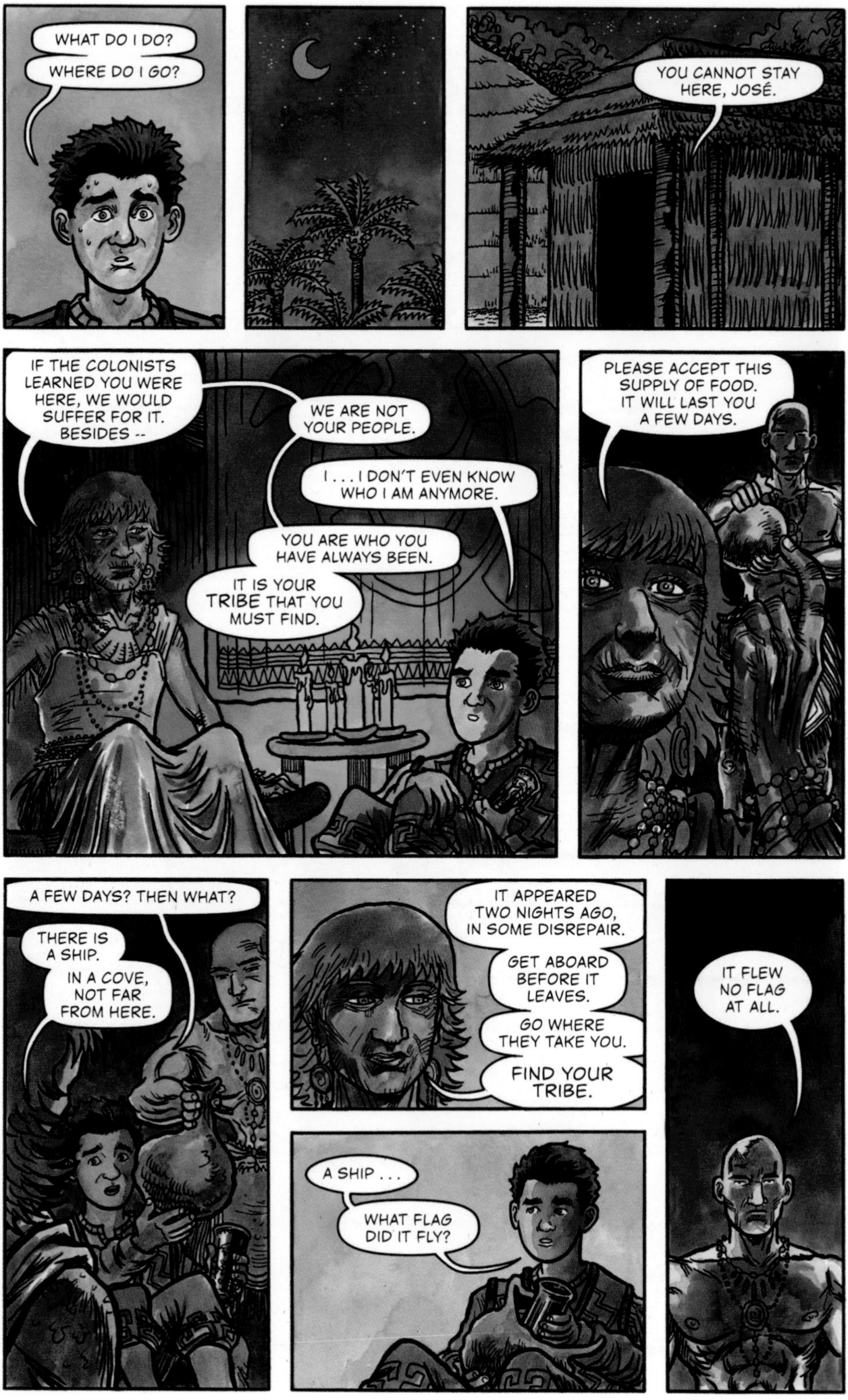
WHAT DO I DO?
WHERE DO I GO?
YOU CANNOT STAY HERE, JOSÉ.
IF THE COLONISTS LEARNED YOU WERE HERE, WE WOULD SUFFER FOR IT. BESIDES --
WE ARE NOT YOUR PEOPLE.
I . . . I DON'T EVEN KNOW WHO I AM ANYMORE.
YOU ARE WHO YOU HAVE ALWAYS BEEN.
IT IS YOUR TRIBE THAT YOU MUST FIND.
PLEASE ACCEPT THIS SUPPLY OF FOOD. IT WILL LAST YOU A FEW DAYS.
A FEW DAYS? THEN WHAT?
THERE IS A SHIP.
IN A COVE, NOT FAR FROM HERE.
IT APPEARED TWO NIGHTS AGO, IN SOME DISREPAIR.
GET ABOARD BEFORE IT LEAVES.
GO WHERE THEY TAKE YOU.
FIND YOUR TRIBE.
A SHIP . . .
WHAT FLAG DID IT FLY?
IT FLEW NO FLAG AT ALL.

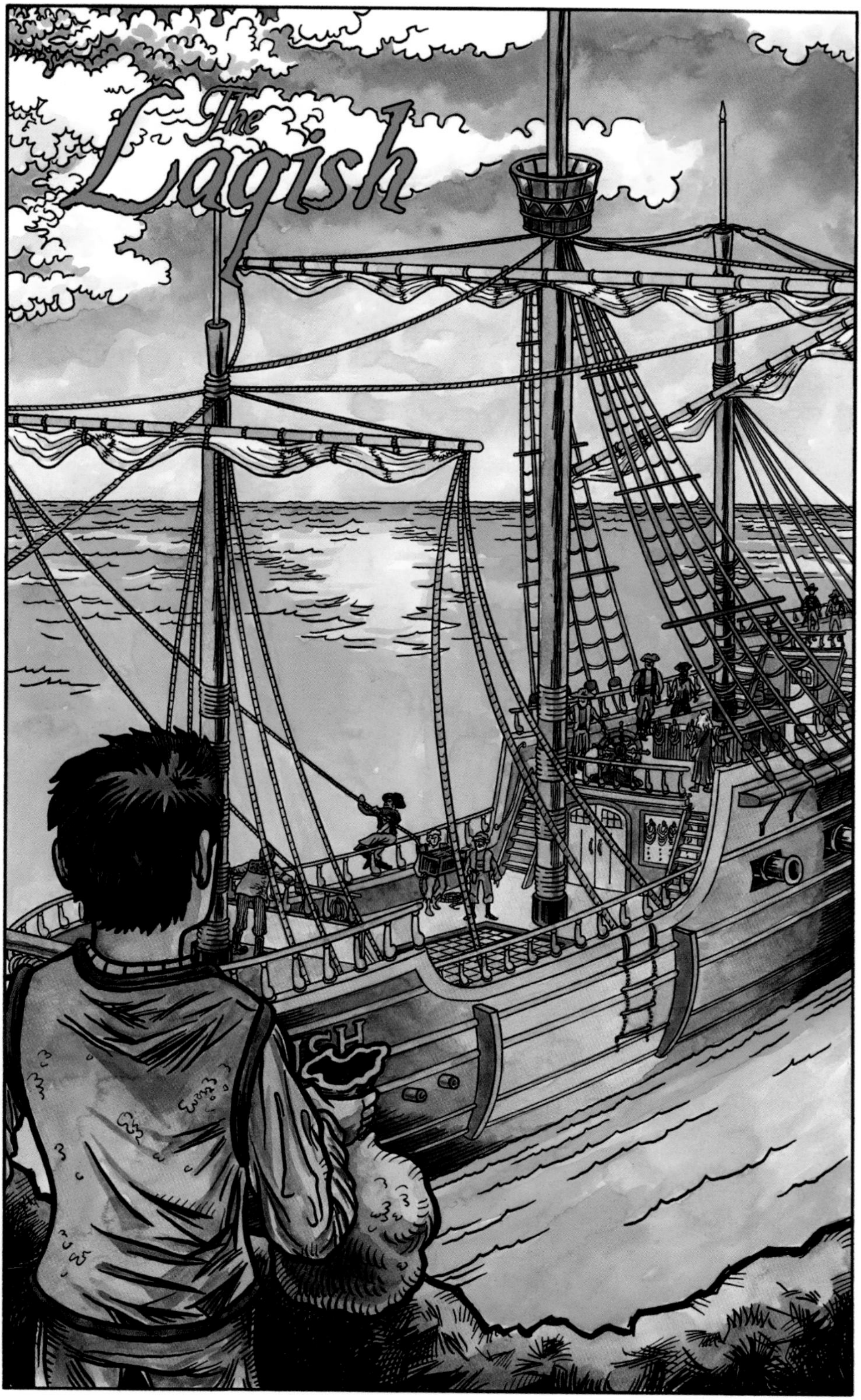
The Laqish

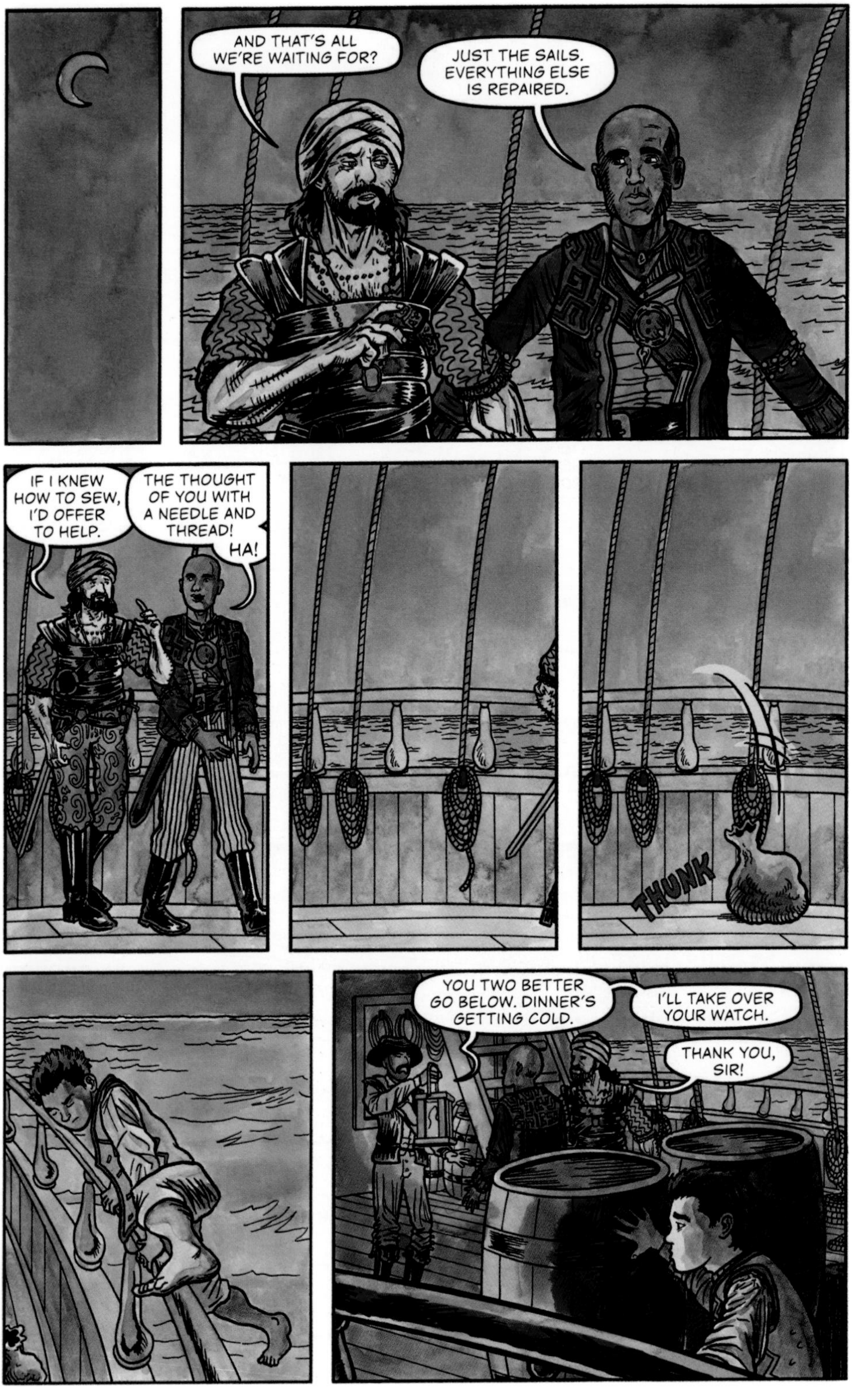
AND THAT'S ALL WE'RE WAITING FOR?
JUST THE SAILS. EVERYTHING ELSE IS REPAIRED.
IF I KNEW HOW TO SEW, I'D OFFER TO HELP.
THE THOUGHT OF YOU WITH A NEEDLE AND THREAD!
HA!
THUNK
YOU TWO BETTER GO BELOW. DINNER'S GETTING COLD.
I'LL TAKE OVER YOUR WATCH.
THANK YOU, SIR!

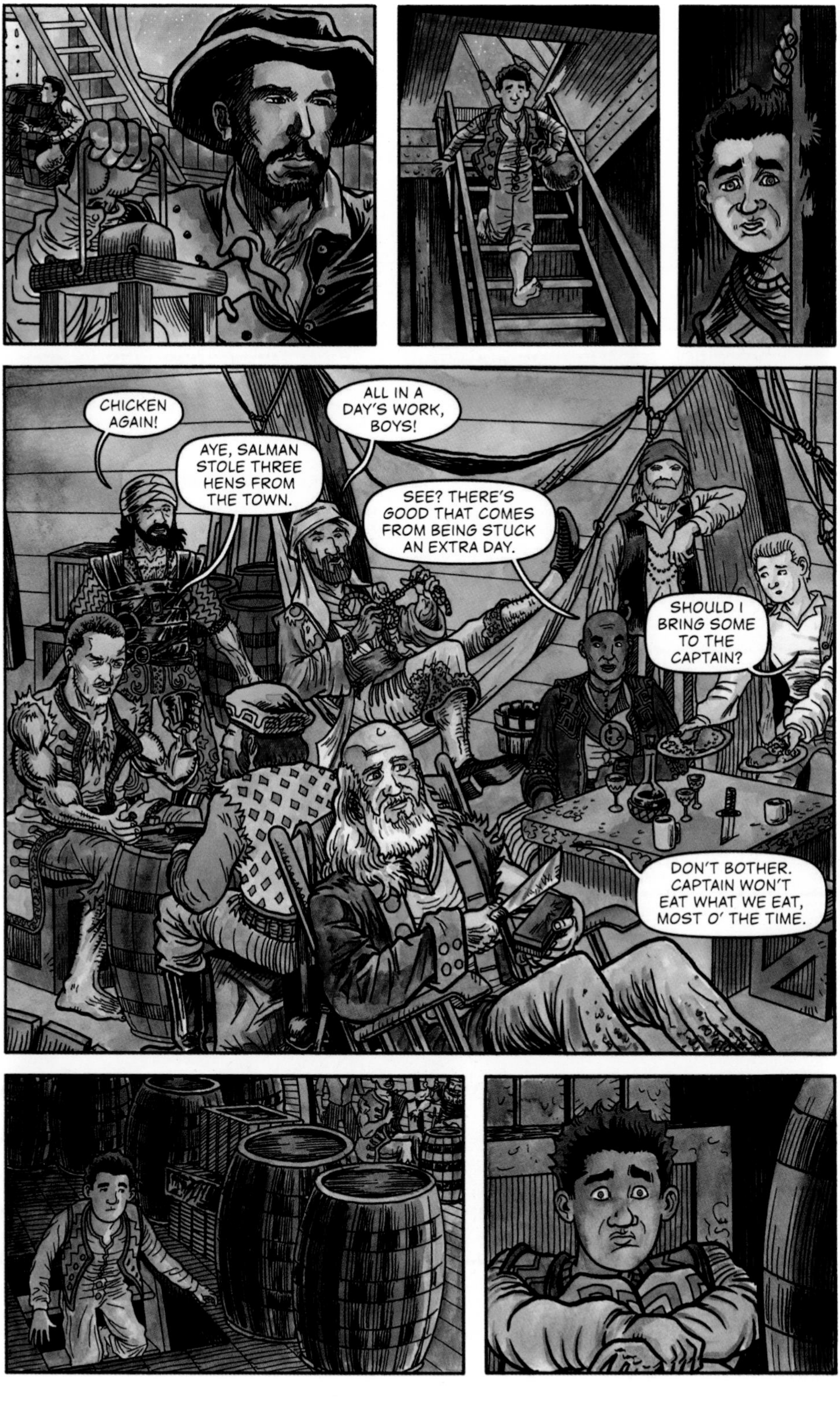
CHICKEN AGAIN!
AYE, SALMAN STOLE THREE HENS FROM THE TOWN.
ALL IN A DAY'S WORK, BOYS!
SEE? THERE'S GOOD THAT COMES FROM BEING STUCK AN EXTRA DAY.
SHOULD I BRING SOME TO THE CAPTAIN?
DON'T BOTHER. CAPTAIN WON'T EAT WHAT WE EAT, MOST O' THE TIME.

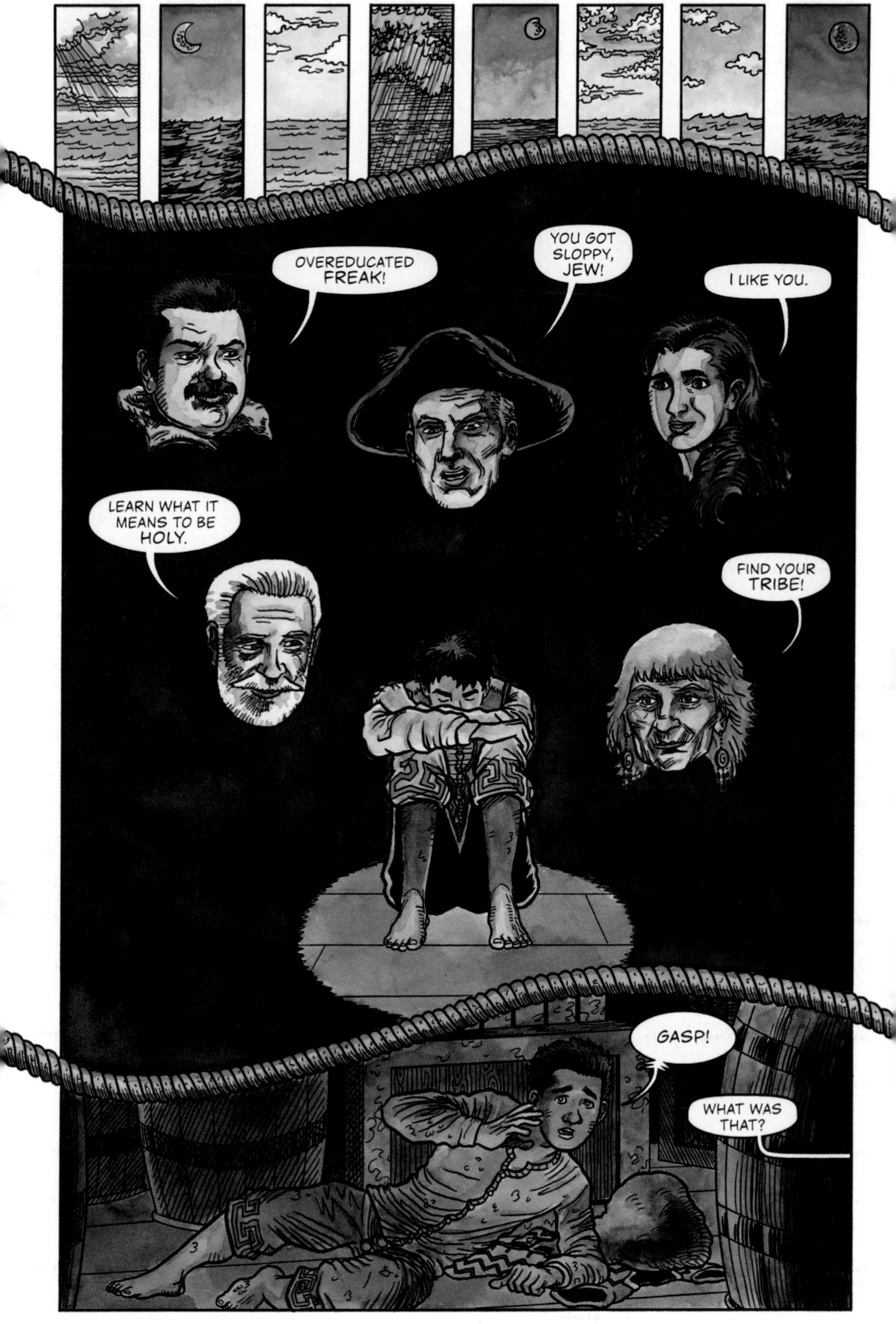
OVEREDUCATED FREAK!
YOU GOT SLOPPY, JEW!
I LIKE YOU.
LEARN WHAT IT MEANS TO BE HOLY.
FIND YOUR TRIBE!
GASP!
WHAT WAS THAT?

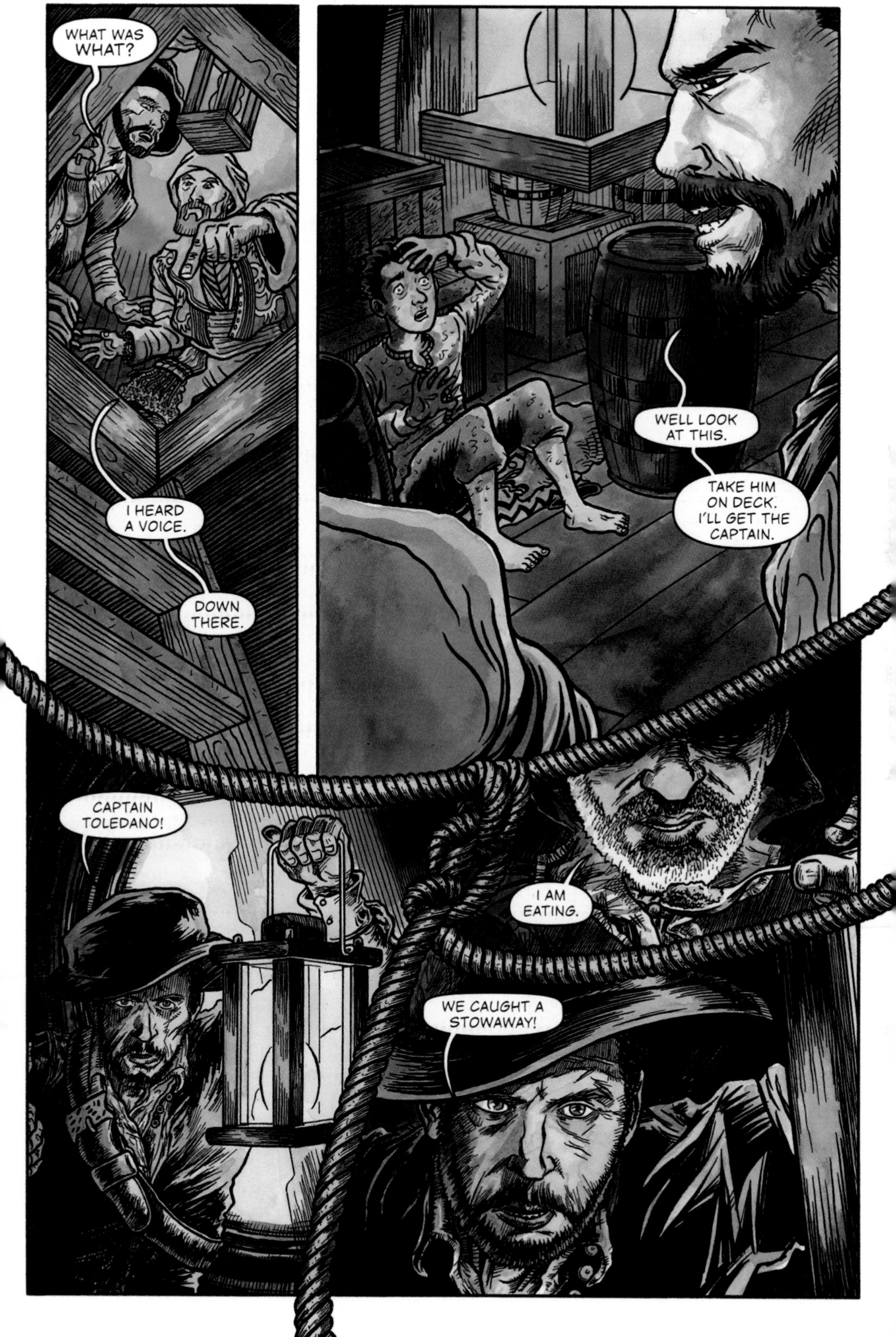
WHAT WAS WHAT?
I HEARD A VOICE.
DOWN THERE.
WELL LOOK AT THIS.
TAKE HIM ON DECK. I'LL GET THE CAPTAIN.
CAPTAIN TOLEDANO!
I AM EATING.
WE CAUGHT A STOWAWAY!

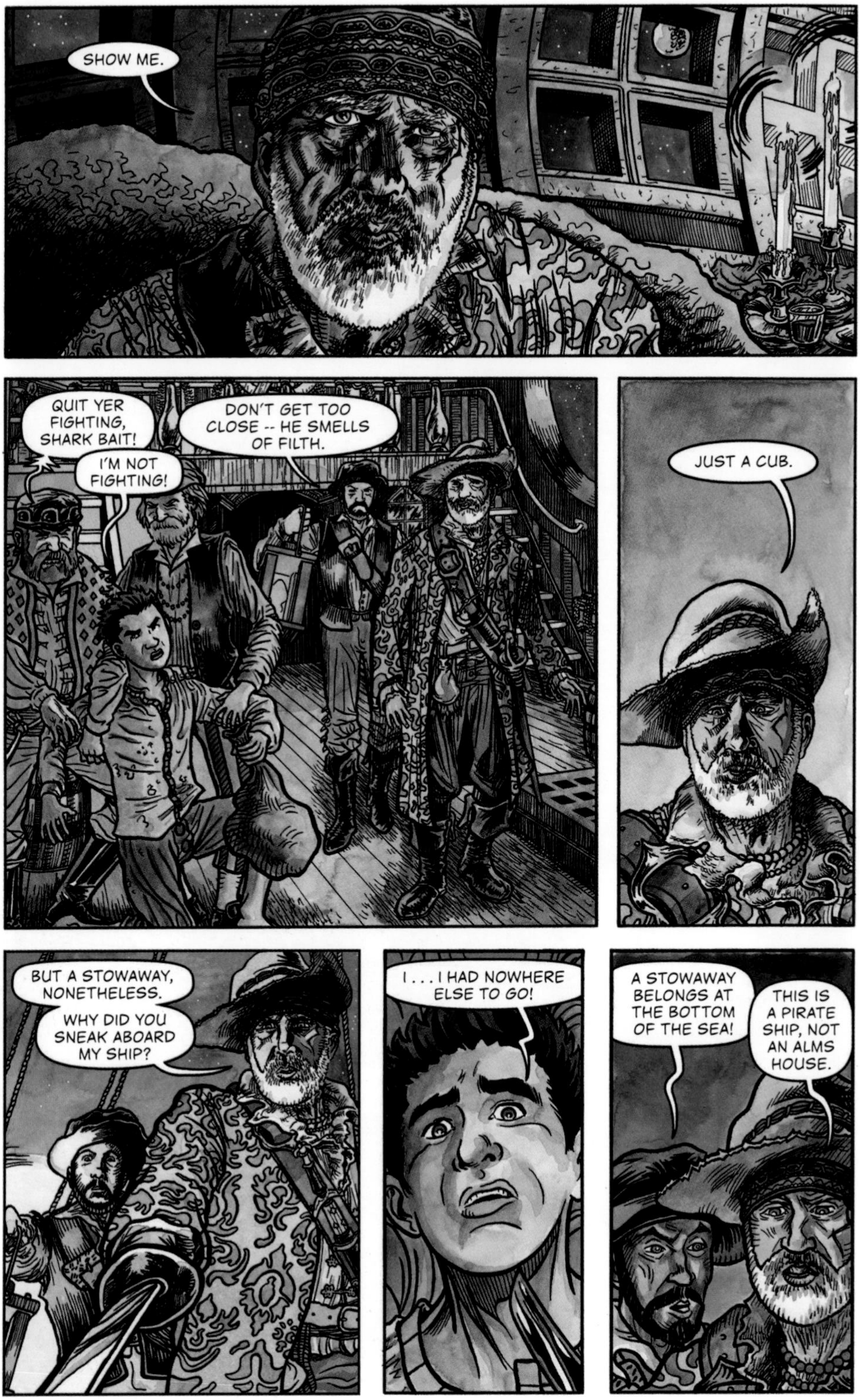
SHOW ME.
QUIT YER FIGHTING, SHARK BAIT!
I'M NOT FIGHTING!
DON'T GET TOO CLOSE -- HE SMELLS OF FILTH.
JUST A CUB.
BUT A STOWAWAY, NONETHELESS.
WHY DID YOU SNEAK ABOARD MY SHIP?
I . . . I HAD NOWHERE ELSE TO GO!
A STOWAWAY BELONGS AT THE BOTTOM OF THE SEA!
THIS IS A PIRATE SHIP, NOT AN ALMS HOUSE.

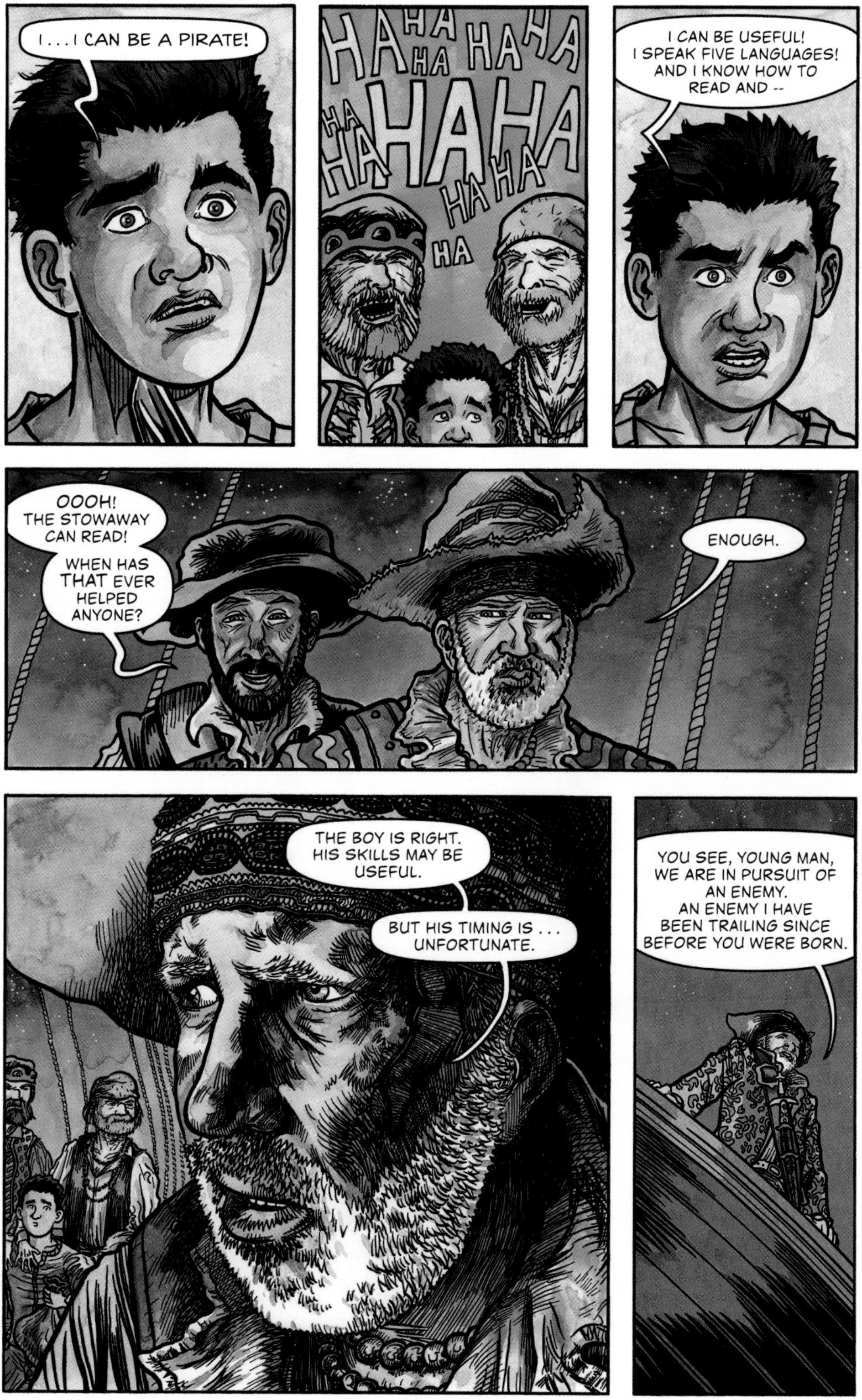
I . . . I CAN BE A PIRATE!
HAHAHAHAHAHA HAHAHAHA HAHAHA HA
I CAN BE USEFUL! I SPEAK FIVE LANGUAGES! AND I KNOW HOW TO READ AND --
OOOH! THE STOWAWAY CAN READ!
WHEN HAS THAT EVER HELPED ANYONE?
ENOUGH.
THE BOY IS RIGHT. HIS SKILLS MAY BE USEFUL.
BUT HIS TIMING IS . . . UNFORTUNATE.
YOU SEE, YOUNG MAN, WE ARE IN PURSUIT OF AN ENEMY. AN ENEMY I HAVE BEEN TRAILING SINCE BEFORE YOU WERE BORN.

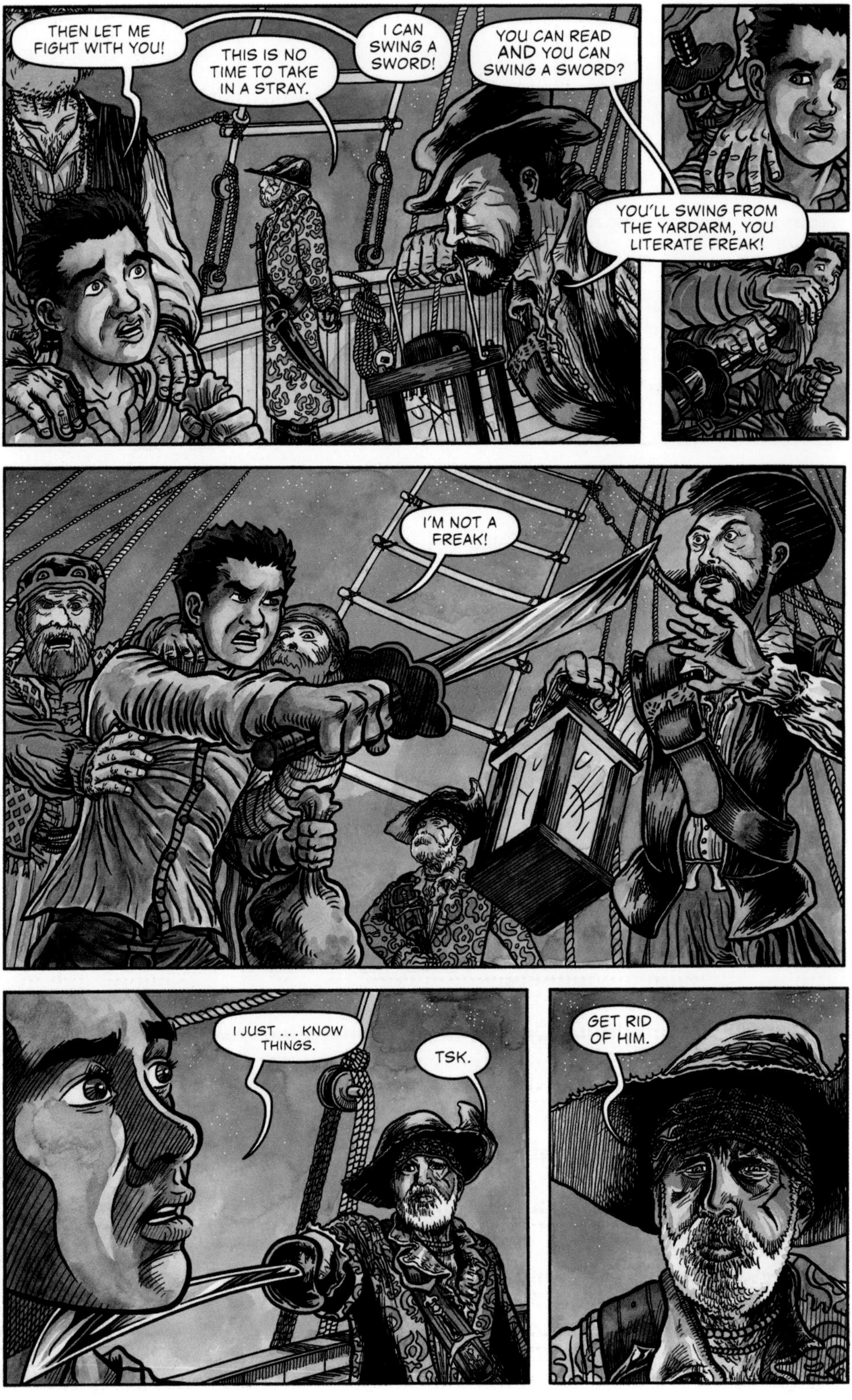
THEN LET ME FIGHT WITH YOU!
THIS IS NO TIME TO TAKE IN A STRAY.
I CAN SWING A SWORD!
YOU CAN READ AND YOU CAN SWING A SWORD?
YOU'LL SWING FROM THE YARDARM, YOU LITERATE FREAK!
I'M NOT A FREAK!
I JUST . . . KNOW THINGS.
TSK.
GET RID OF HIM.

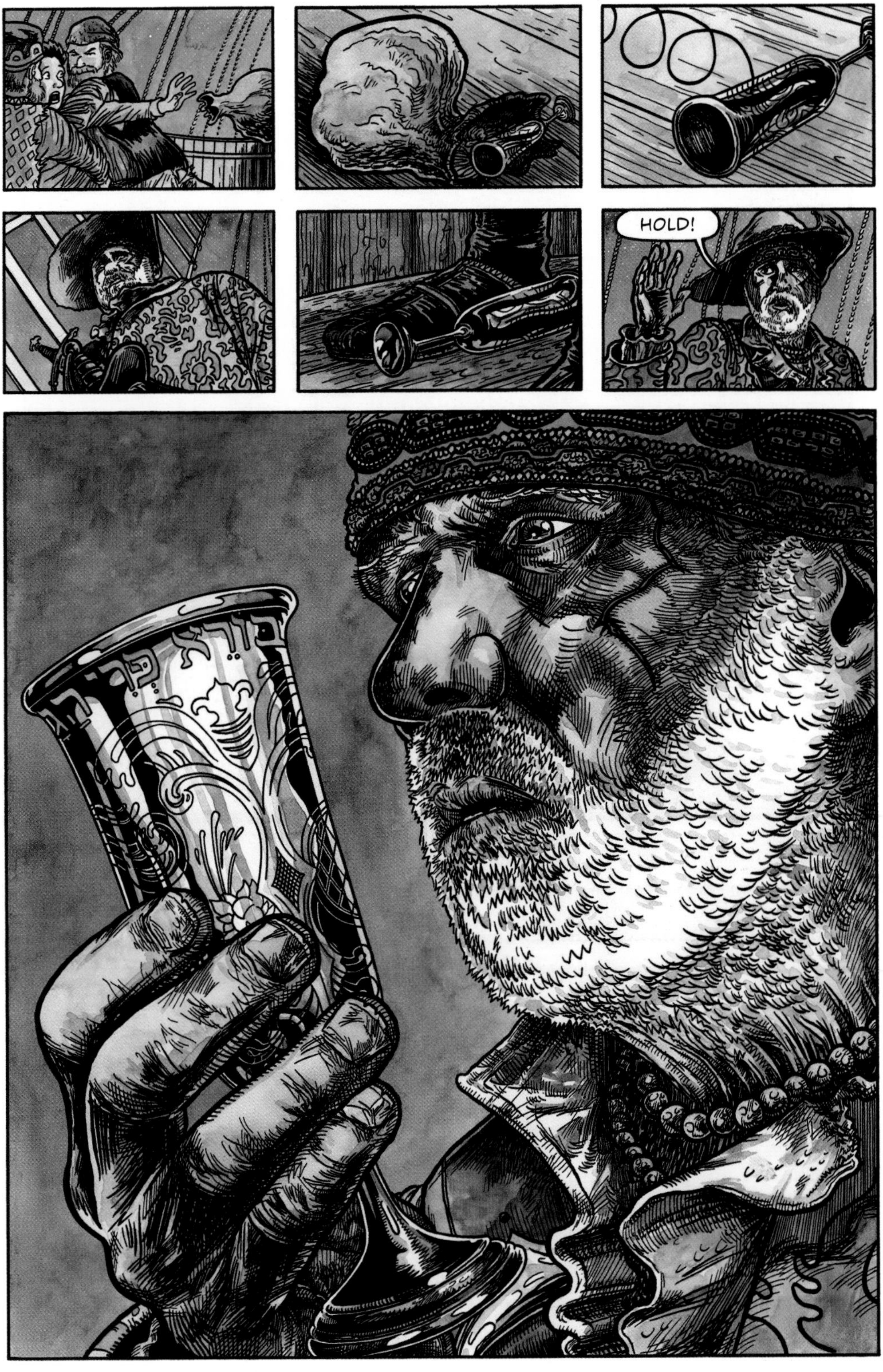
HOLD!

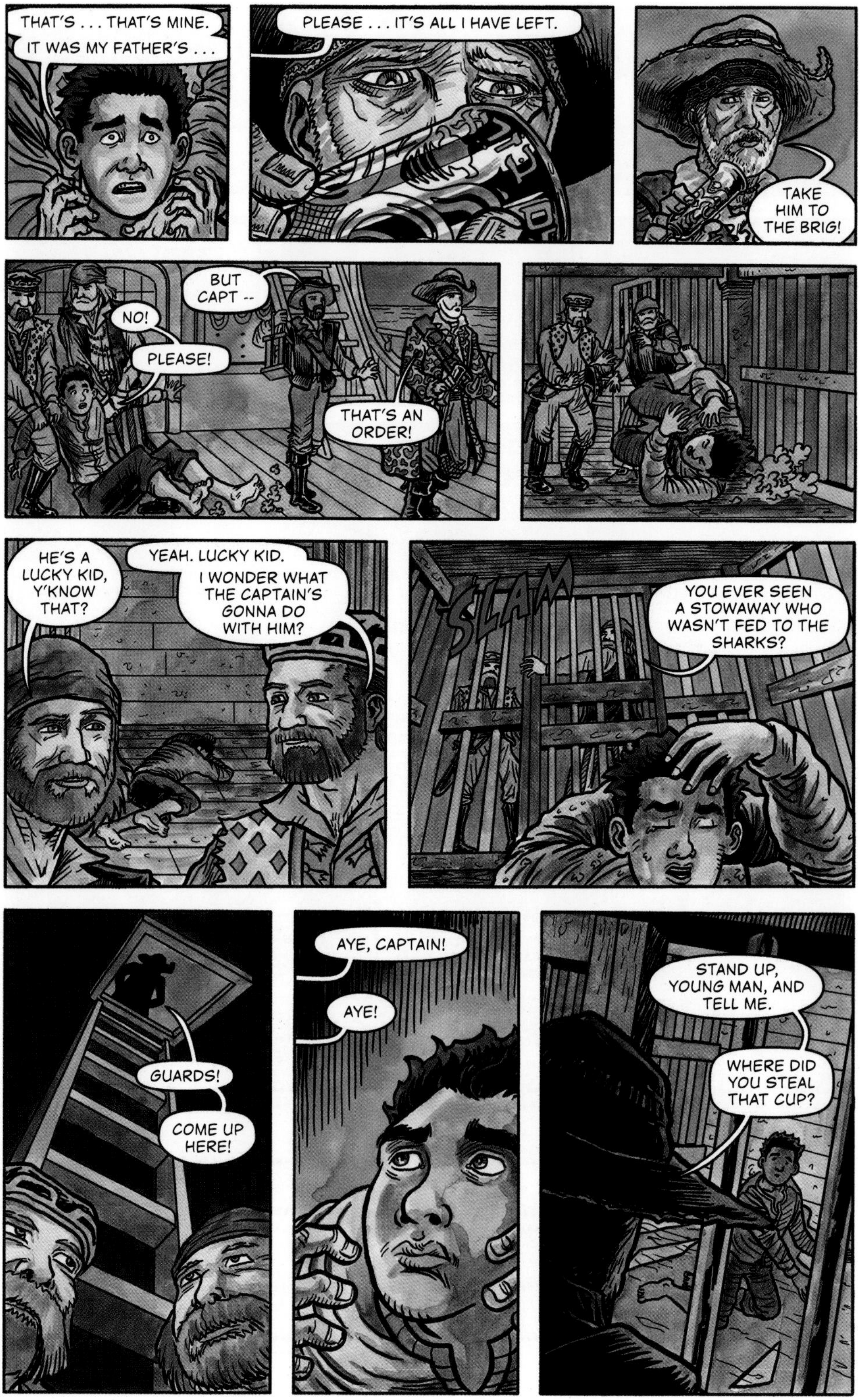
THAT'S . . . THAT'S MINE.
IT WAS MY FATHER'S . . .
PLEASE . . . IT'S ALL I HAVE LEFT.
TAKE HIM TO THE BRIG!
BUT CAPT --
NO!
PLEASE!
THAT'S AN ORDER!
HE'S A LUCKY KID, Y'KNOW THAT?
YEAH. LUCKY KID.
I WONDER WHAT THE CAPTAIN'S GONNA DO WITH HIM?
SLAM
YOU EVER SEEN A STOWAWAY WHO WASN'T FED TO THE SHARKS?
GUARDS!
COME UP HERE!
AYE, CAPTAIN!
AYE!
STAND UP, YOUNG MAN, AND TELL ME.
WHERE DID YOU STEAL THAT CUP?

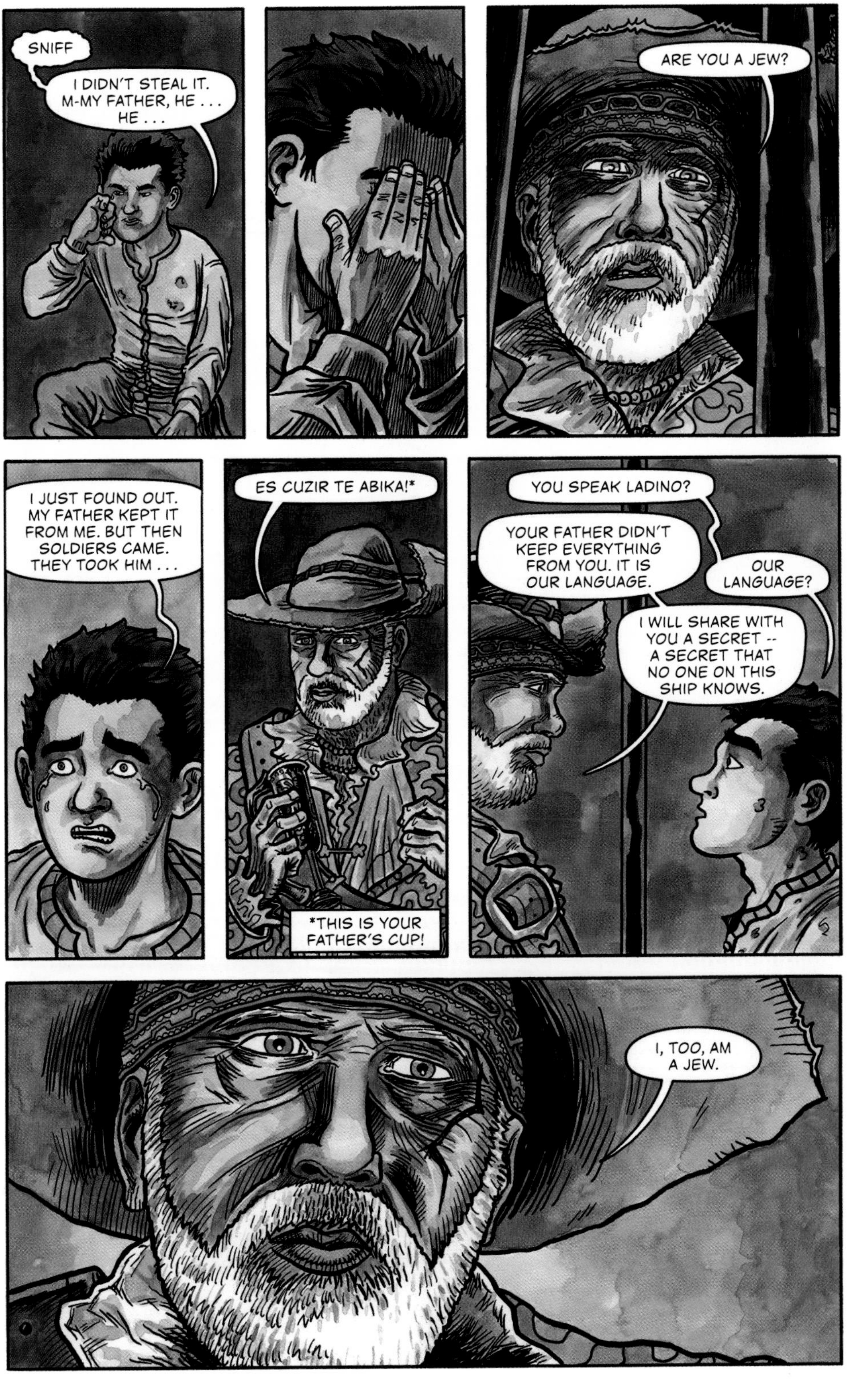
SNIFF
I DIDN'T STEAL IT. M-MY FATHER, HE . . . HE . . .
ARE YOU A JEW?
I JUST FOUND OUT. MY FATHER KEPT IT FROM ME. BUT THEN SOLDIERS CAME. THEY TOOK HIM . . .
ES CUZIR TE ABIKA!*
*THIS IS YOUR FATHER'S CUP!
YOU SPEAK LADINO?
YOUR FATHER DIDN'T KEEP EVERYTHING FROM YOU. IT IS OUR LANGUAGE.
OUR LANGUAGE?
I WILL SHARE WITH YOU A SECRET -- A SECRET THAT NO ONE ON THIS SHIP KNOWS.
I, TOO, AM A JEW.

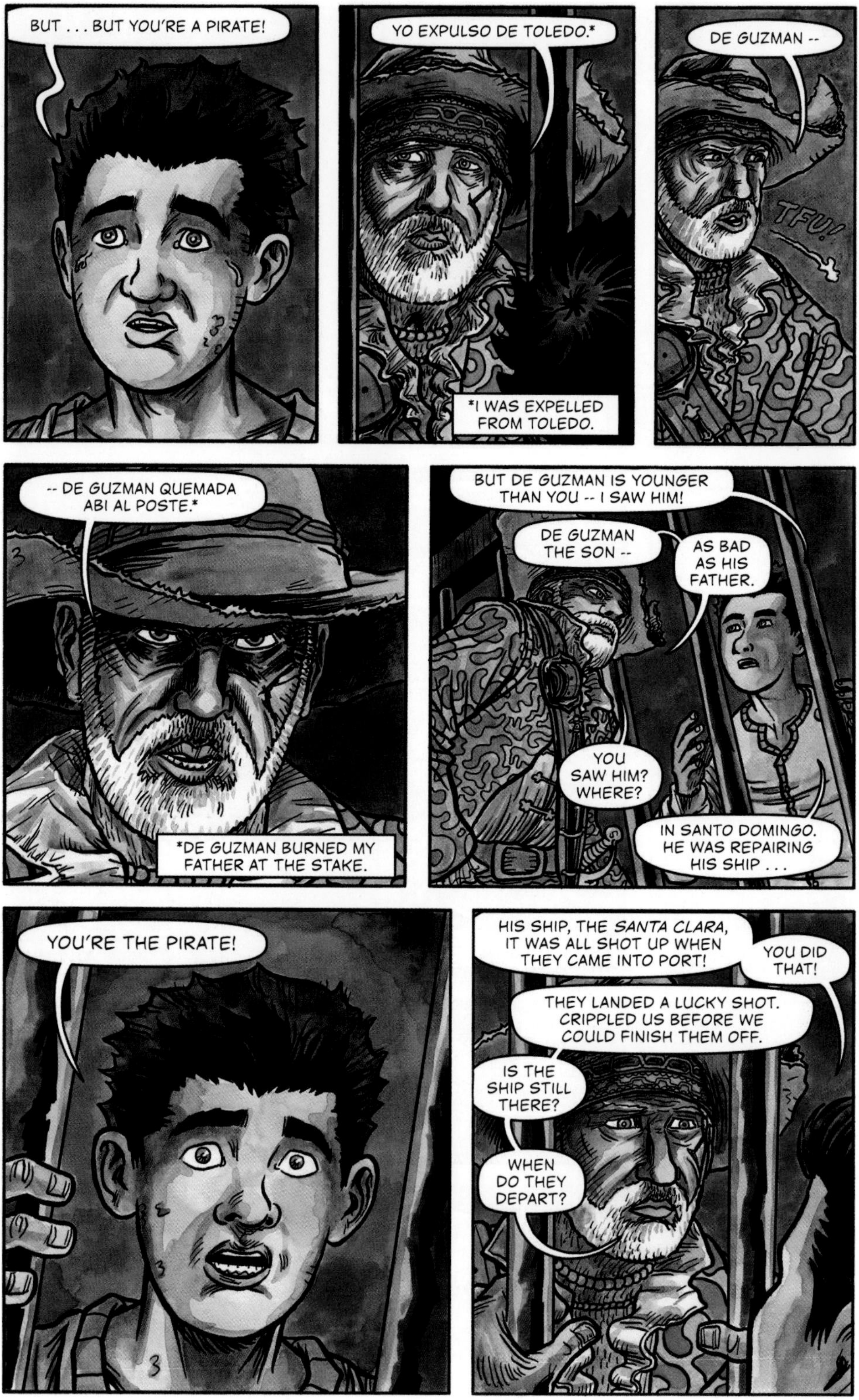

BUT . . . BUT YOU'RE A PIRATE!
YO EXPULSO DE TOLEDO.*
*I WAS EXPELLED FROM TOLEDO.
DE GUZMAN --
TFU!
-- DE GUZMAN QUEMADA ABI AL POSTE.*
*DE GUZMAN BURNED MY FATHER AT THE STAKE.
BUT DE GUZMAN IS YOUNGER THAN YOU -- I SAW HIM!
DE GUZMAN THE SON --
AS BAD AS HIS FATHER.
YOU SAW HIM? WHERE?
IN SANTO DOMINGO. HE WAS REPAIRING HIS SHIP . . .
YOU'RE THE PIRATE!
HIS SHIP, THE *SANTA CLARA*, IT WAS ALL SHOT UP WHEN THEY CAME INTO PORT!
YOU DID THAT!
THEY LANDED A LUCKY SHOT. CRIPPLED US BEFORE WE COULD FINISH THEM OFF.
IS THE SHIP STILL THERE?
WHEN DO THEY DEPART?

41

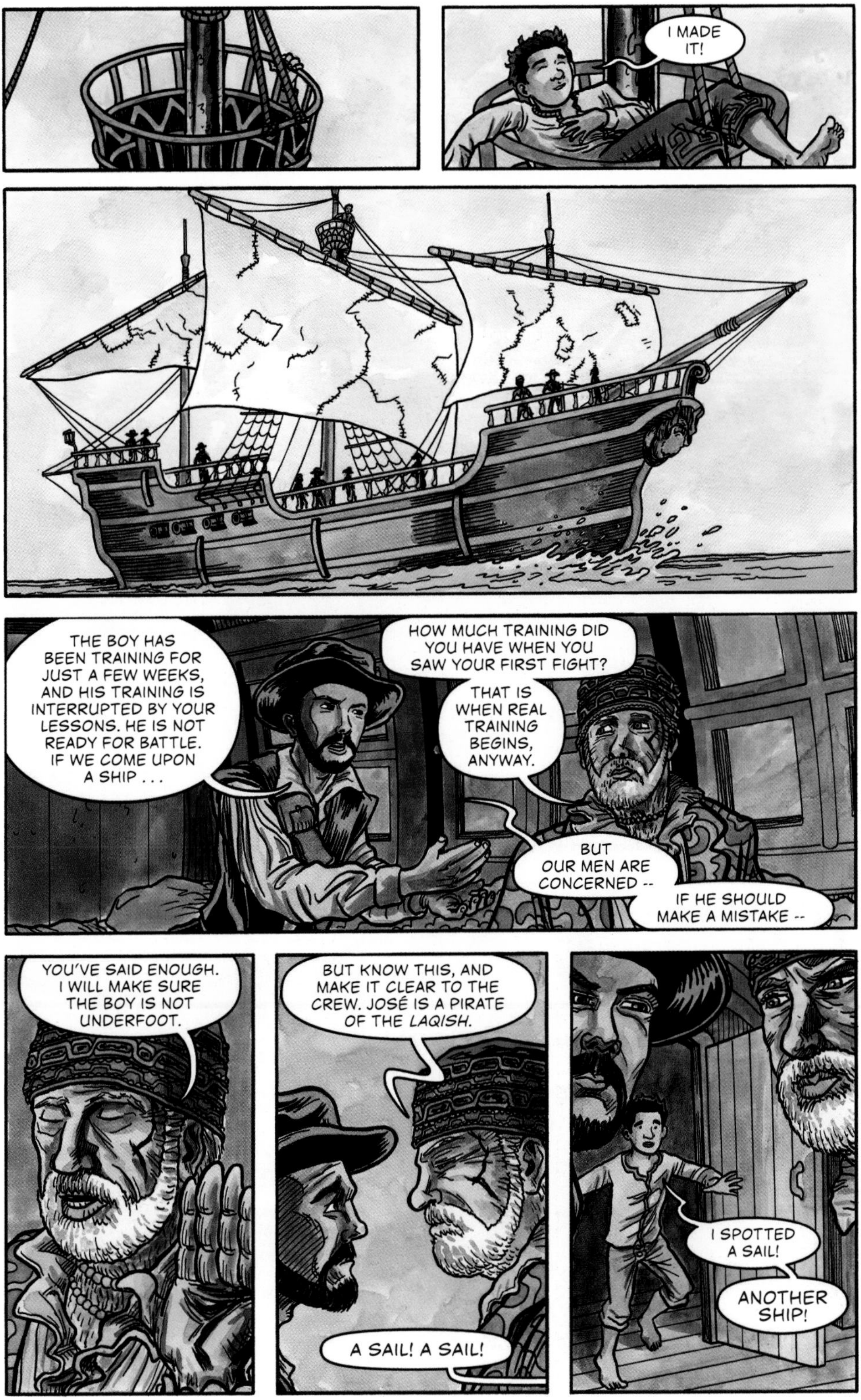
I MADE IT!
THE BOY HAS BEEN TRAINING FOR JUST A FEW WEEKS, AND HIS TRAINING IS INTERRUPTED BY YOUR LESSONS. HE IS NOT READY FOR BATTLE. IF WE COME UPON A SHIP . . .
HOW MUCH TRAINING DID YOU HAVE WHEN YOU SAW YOUR FIRST FIGHT?
THAT IS WHEN REAL TRAINING BEGINS, ANYWAY.
BUT OUR MEN ARE CONCERNED --
IF HE SHOULD MAKE A MISTAKE --
YOU'VE SAID ENOUGH. I WILL MAKE SURE THE BOY IS NOT UNDERFOOT.
BUT KNOW THIS, AND MAKE IT CLEAR TO THE CREW. JOSÉ IS A PIRATE OF THE *LAQISH*.
A SAIL! A SAIL!
I SPOTTED A SAIL!
ANOTHER SHIP!

44

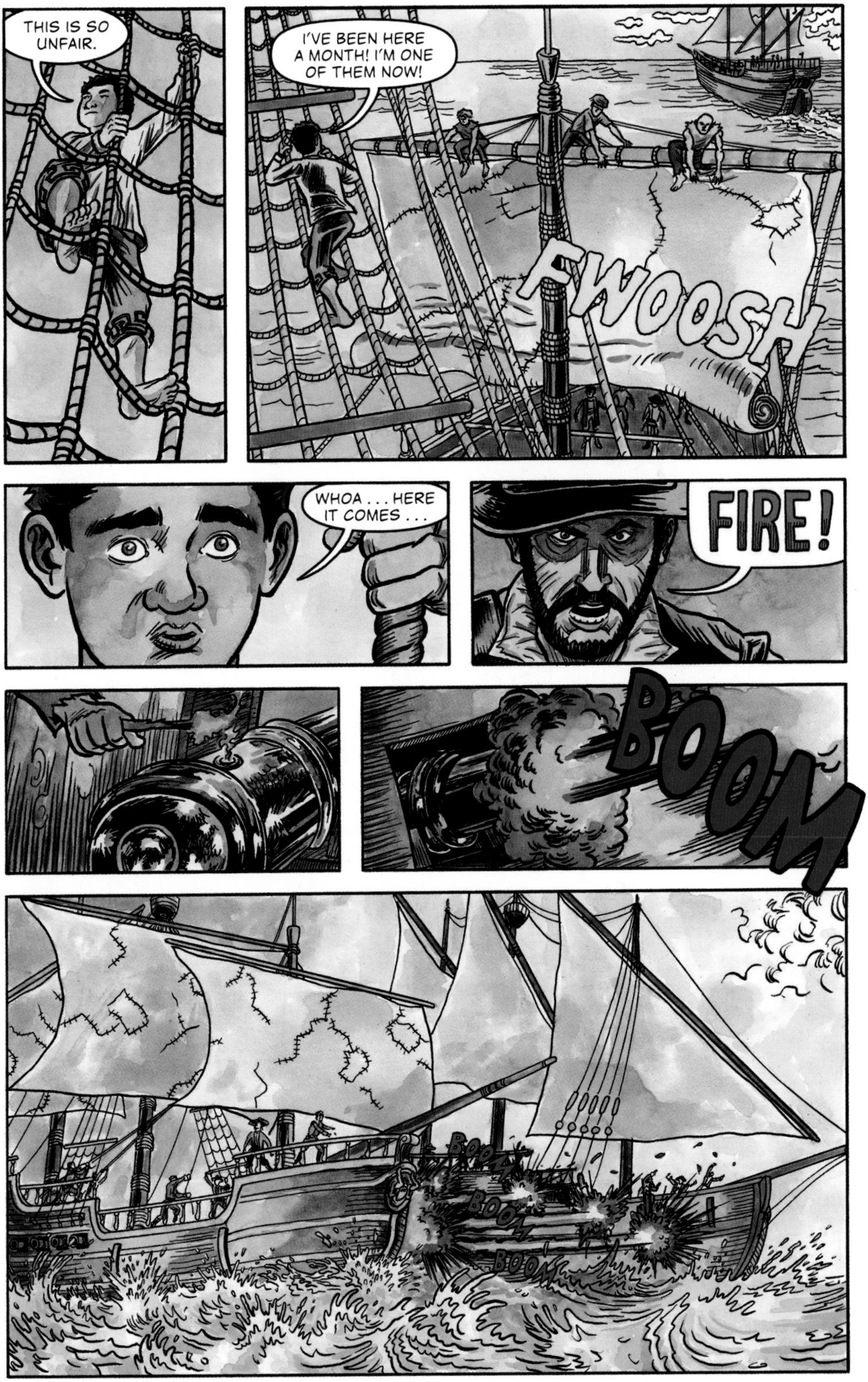
THIS IS SO UNFAIR.
I'VE BEEN HERE A MONTH! I'M ONE OF THEM NOW!
FWOOSH
WHOA . . . HERE IT COMES . . .
FIRE!
BOOM
BOOM
BOOM
BOOM

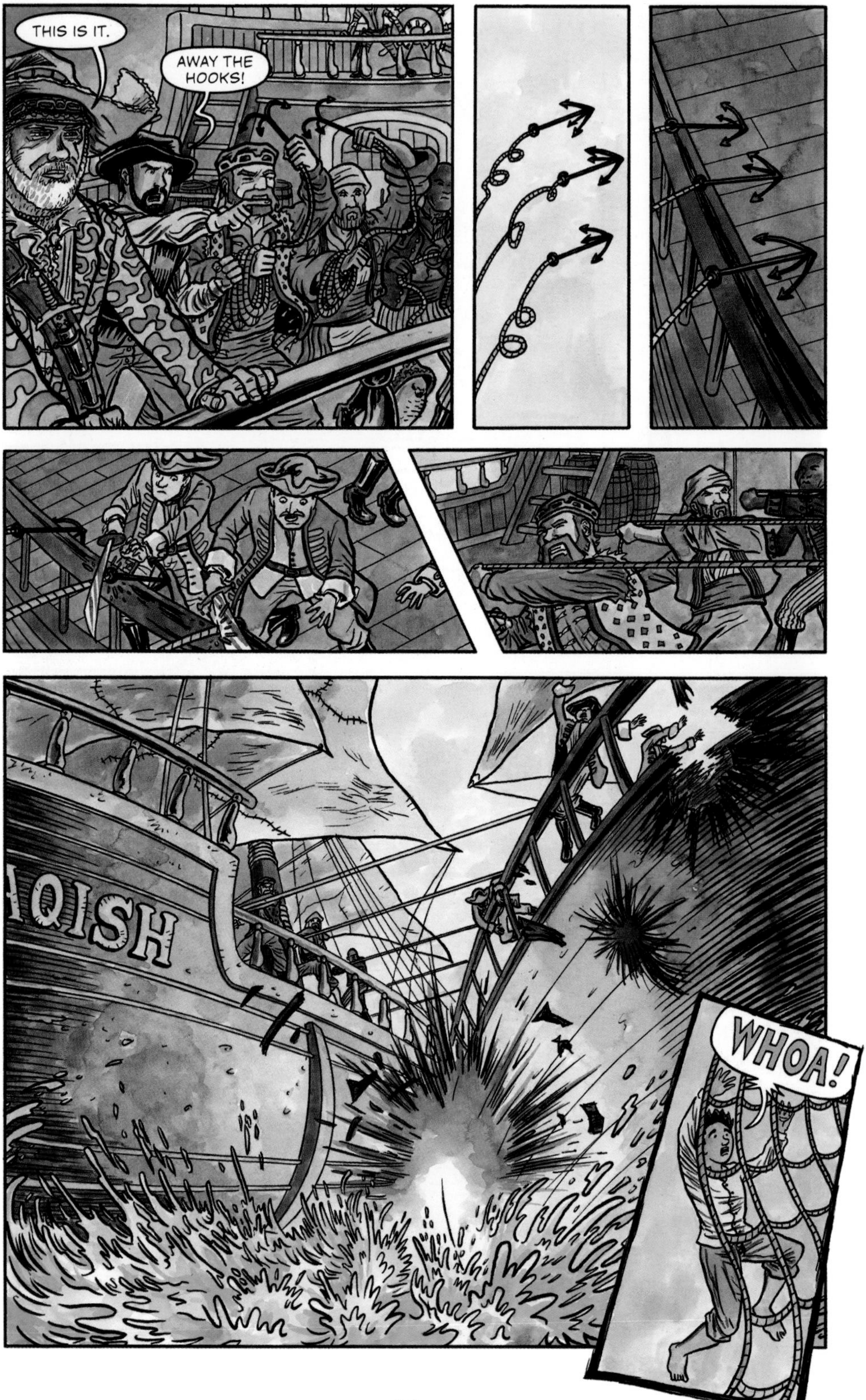
THIS IS IT.
AWAY THE HOOKS!
AQISH
WHOA!

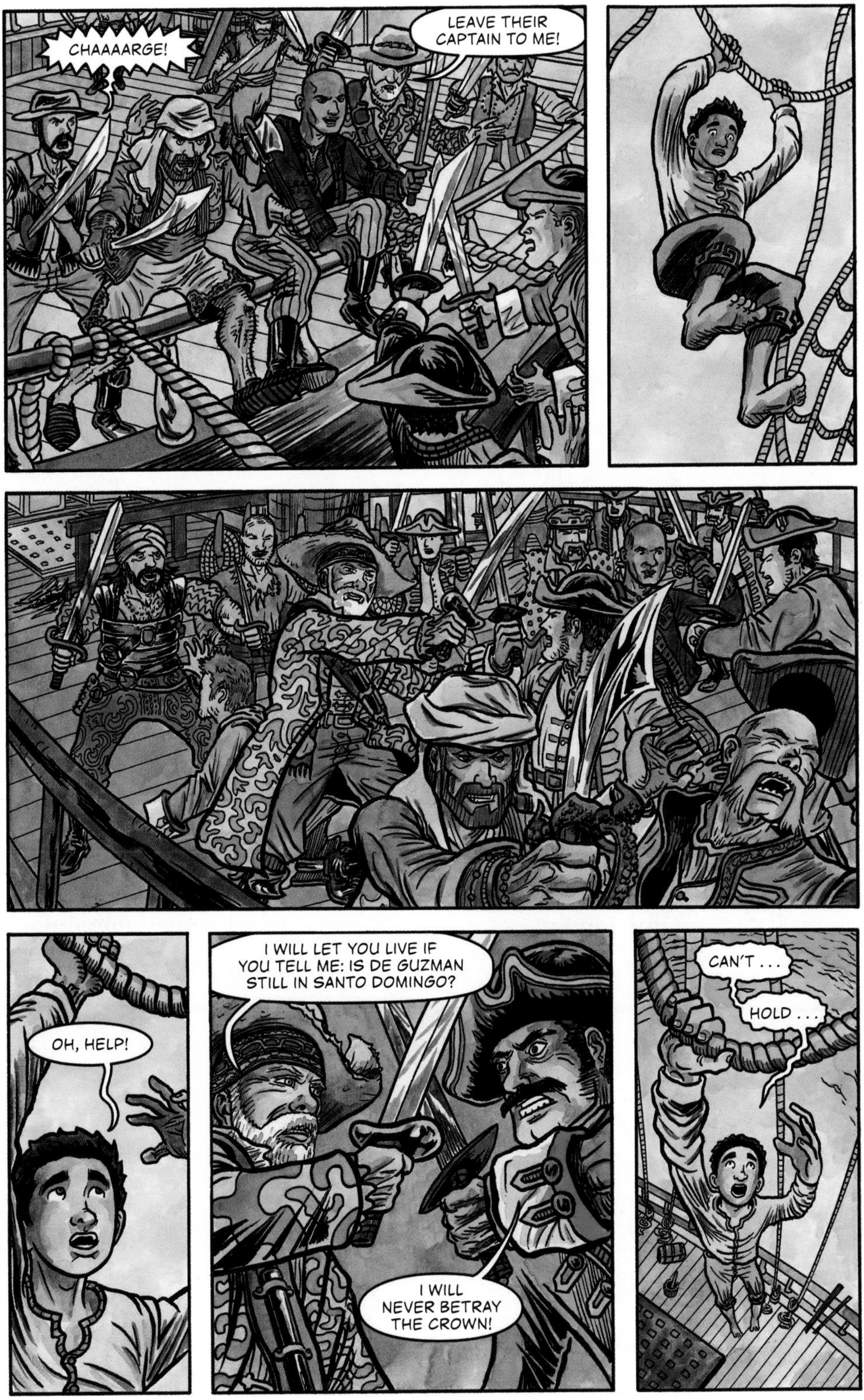
CHAAAARGE!
LEAVE THEIR CAPTAIN TO ME!
OH, HELP!
I WILL LET YOU LIVE IF YOU TELL ME: IS DE GUZMAN STILL IN SANTO DOMINGO?
I WILL NEVER BETRAY THE CROWN!
CAN'T . . .
HOLD . . .

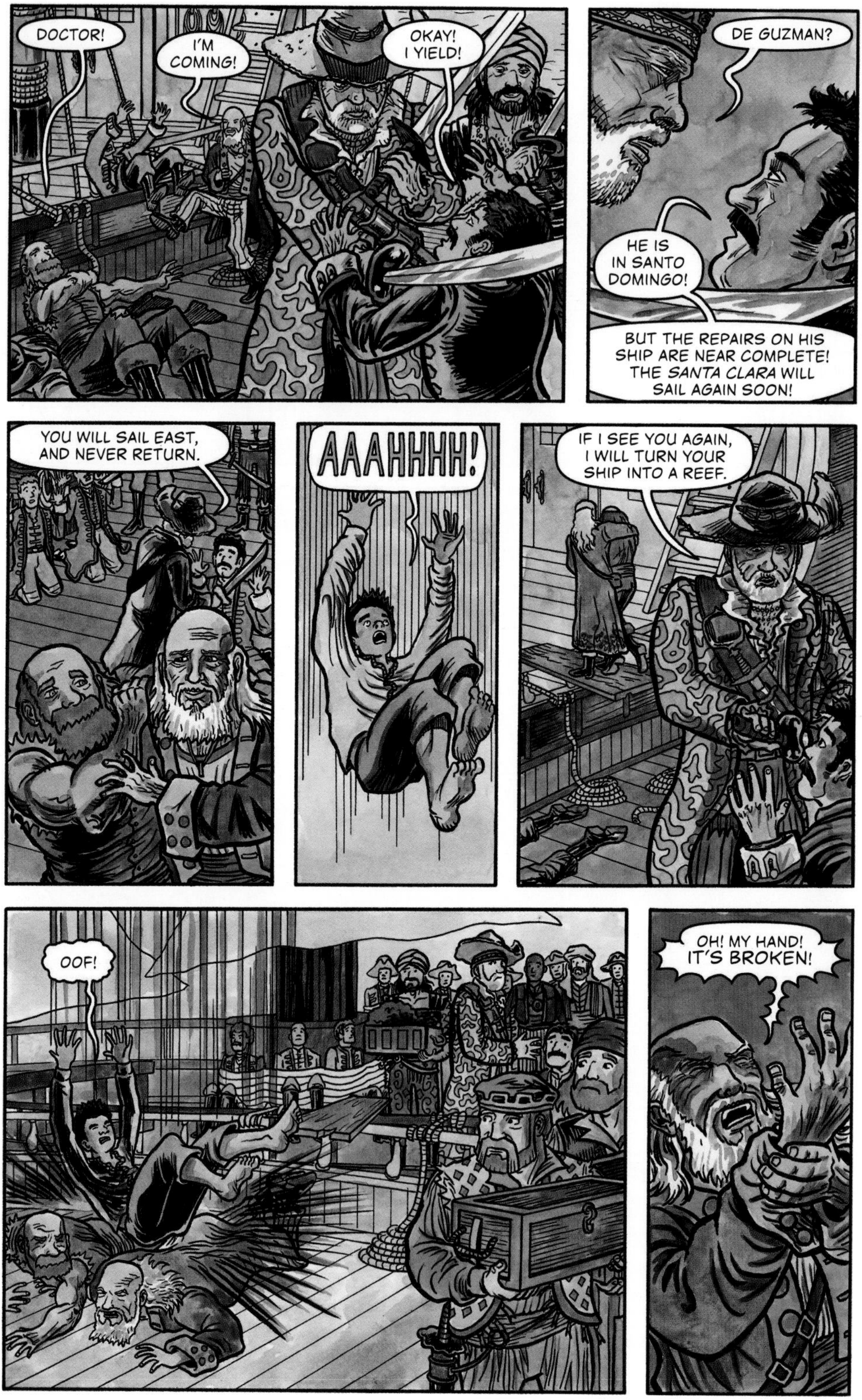

DOCTOR!
I'M COMING!
OKAY! I YIELD!
DE GUZMAN?
HE IS IN SANTO DOMINGO!
BUT THE REPAIRS ON HIS SHIP ARE NEAR COMPLETE! THE *SANTA CLARA* WILL SAIL AGAIN SOON!
YOU WILL SAIL EAST, AND NEVER RETURN.
AAAHHHH!
IF I SEE YOU AGAIN, I WILL TURN YOUR SHIP INTO A REEF.
OOF!
OH! MY HAND! IT'S BROKEN!

49

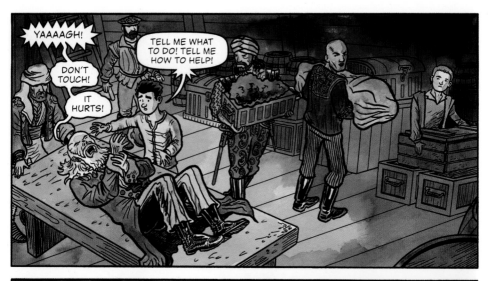

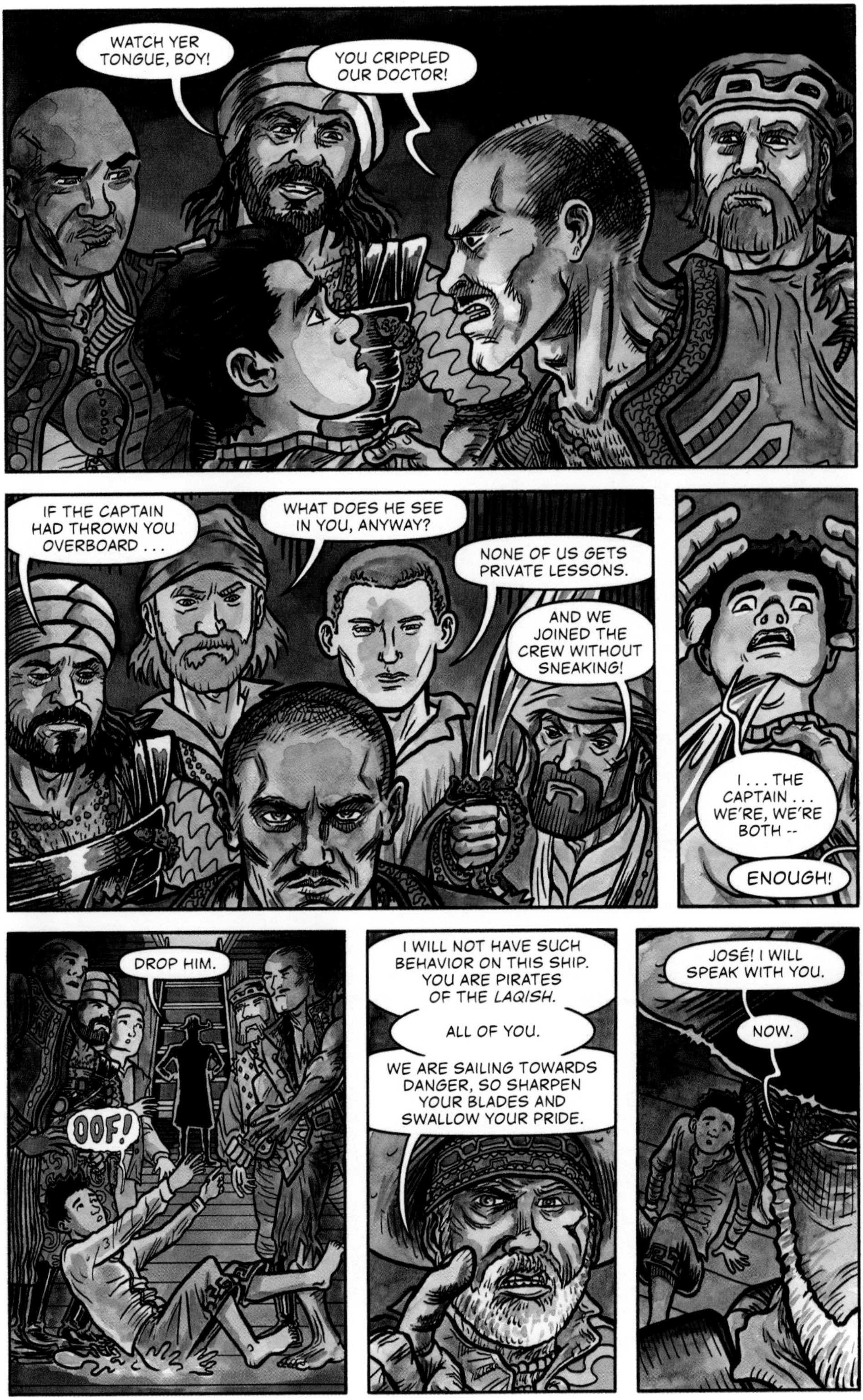
WATCH YER TONGUE, BOY!
YOU CRIPPLED OUR DOCTOR!
IF THE CAPTAIN HAD THROWN YOU OVERBOARD . . .
WHAT DOES HE SEE IN YOU, ANYWAY?
NONE OF US GETS PRIVATE LESSONS.
AND WE JOINED THE CREW WITHOUT SNEAKING!
I . . . THE CAPTAIN . . . WE'RE, WE'RE BOTH --
ENOUGH!
DROP HIM.
OOF!
I WILL NOT HAVE SUCH BEHAVIOR ON THIS SHIP. YOU ARE PIRATES OF THE *LAQISH*.
ALL OF YOU.
WE ARE SAILING TOWARDS DANGER, SO SHARPEN YOUR BLADES AND SWALLOW YOUR PRIDE.
JOSÉ! I WILL SPEAK WITH YOU.
NOW.

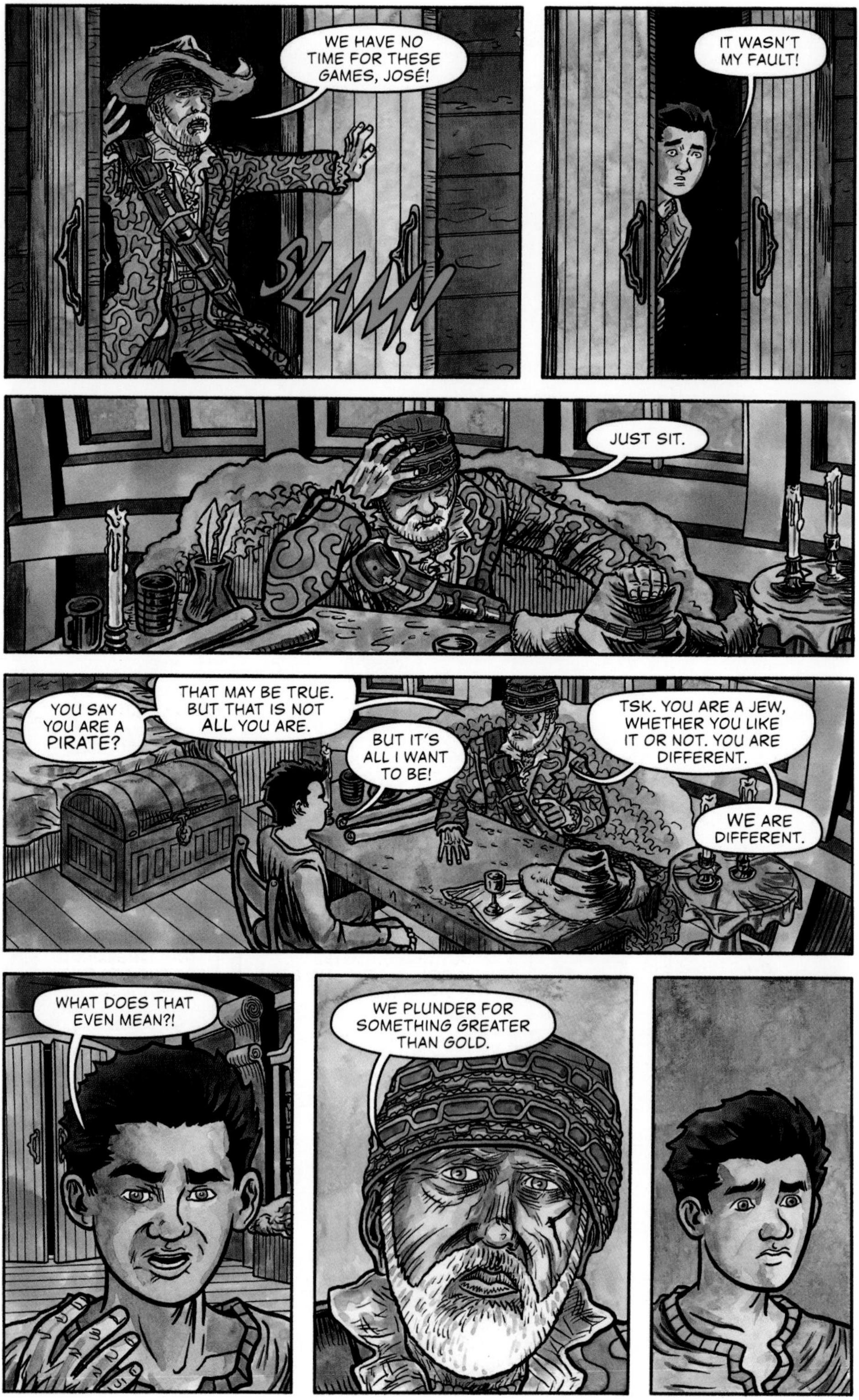
WE HAVE NO TIME FOR THESE GAMES, JOSÉ!
SLAM!
IT WASN'T MY FAULT!
JUST SIT.
YOU SAY YOU ARE A PIRATE?
THAT MAY BE TRUE. BUT THAT IS NOT ALL YOU ARE.
BUT IT'S ALL I WANT TO BE!
TSK. YOU ARE A JEW, WHETHER YOU LIKE IT OR NOT. YOU ARE DIFFERENT.
WE ARE DIFFERENT.
WHAT DOES THAT EVEN MEAN?!
WE PLUNDER FOR SOMETHING GREATER THAN GOLD.

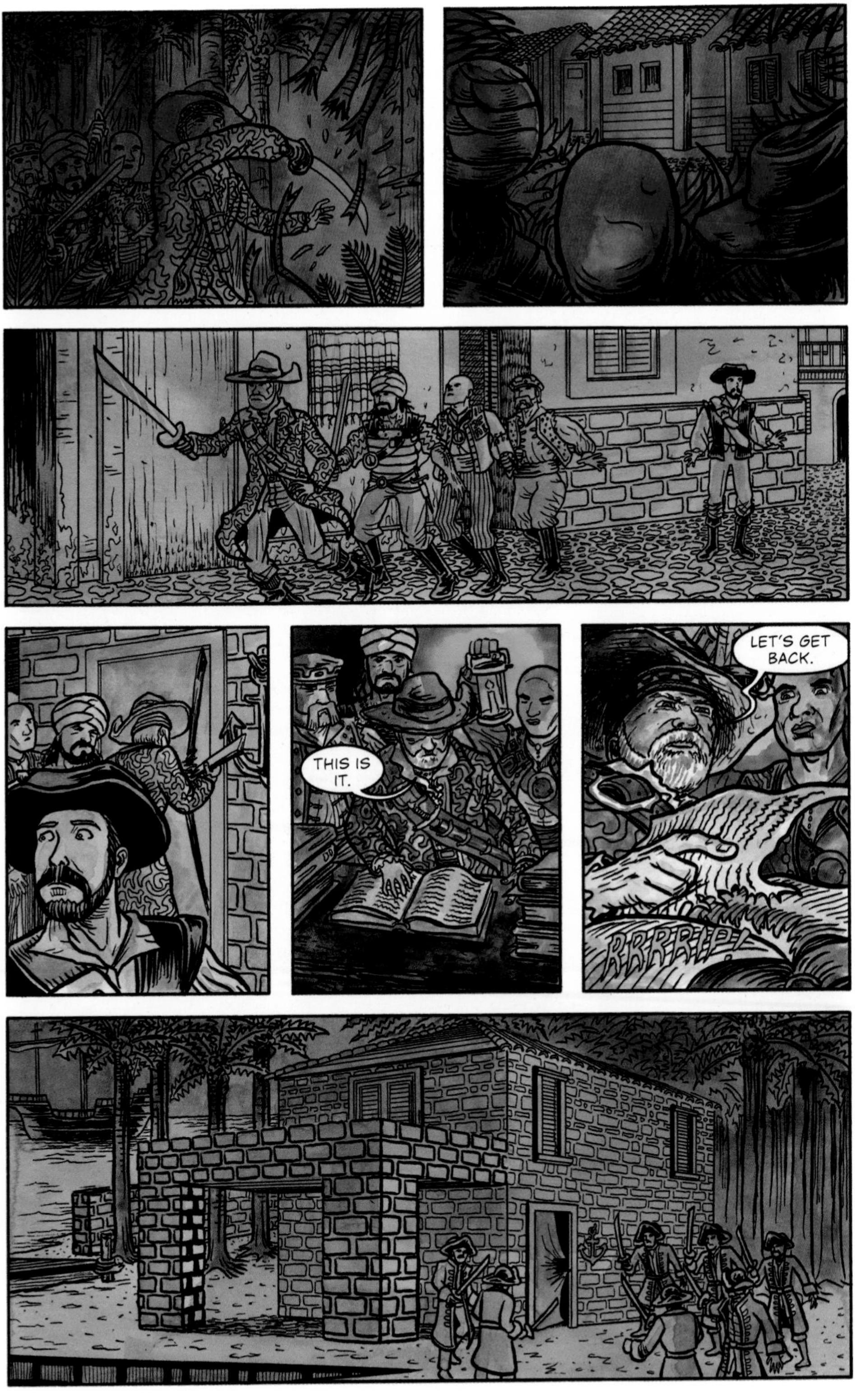
THIS IS IT.
LET'S GET BACK.
RRRRIP!

65

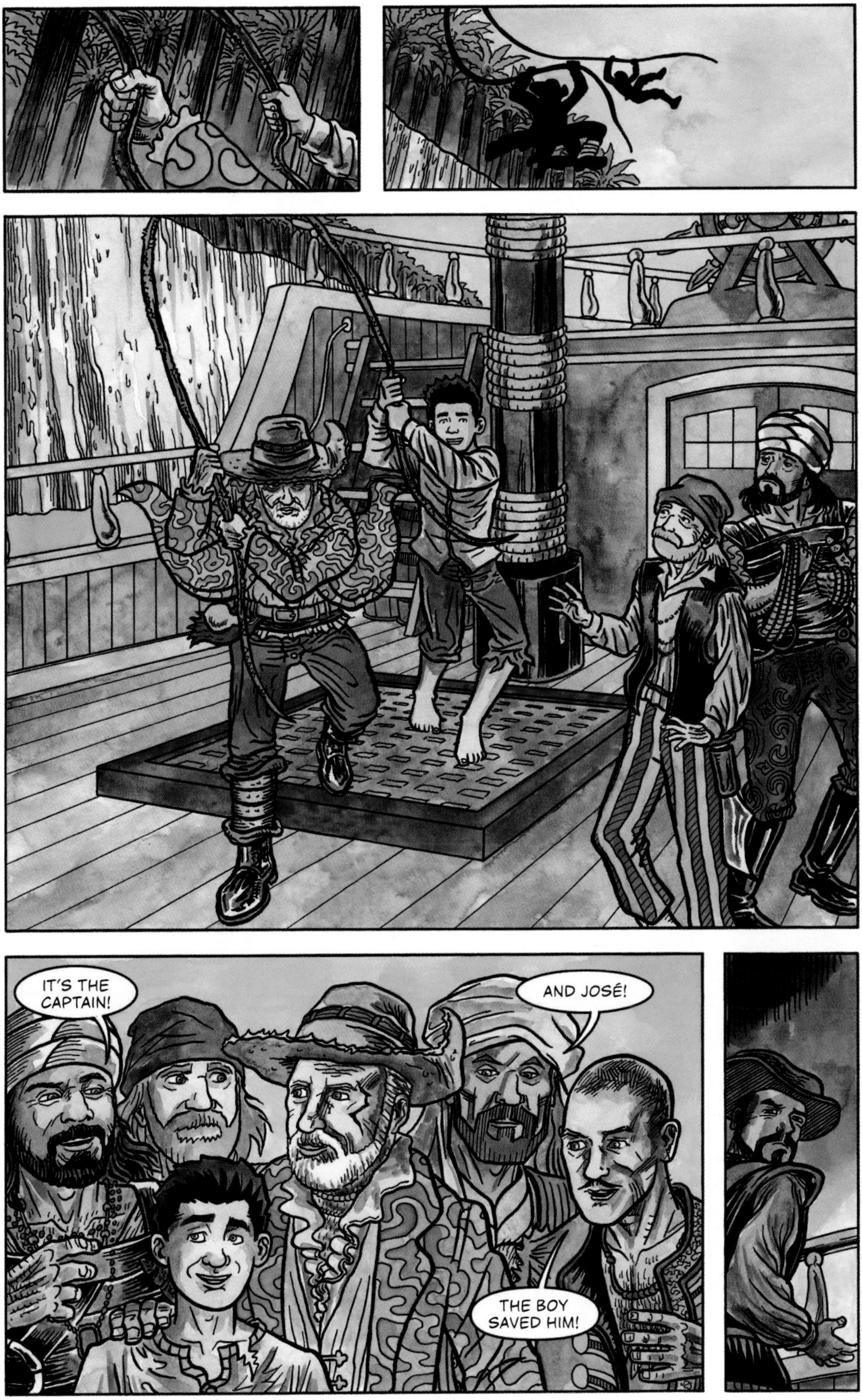
IT'S THE CAPTAIN!
AND JOSÉ!
THE BOY SAVED HIM!

70

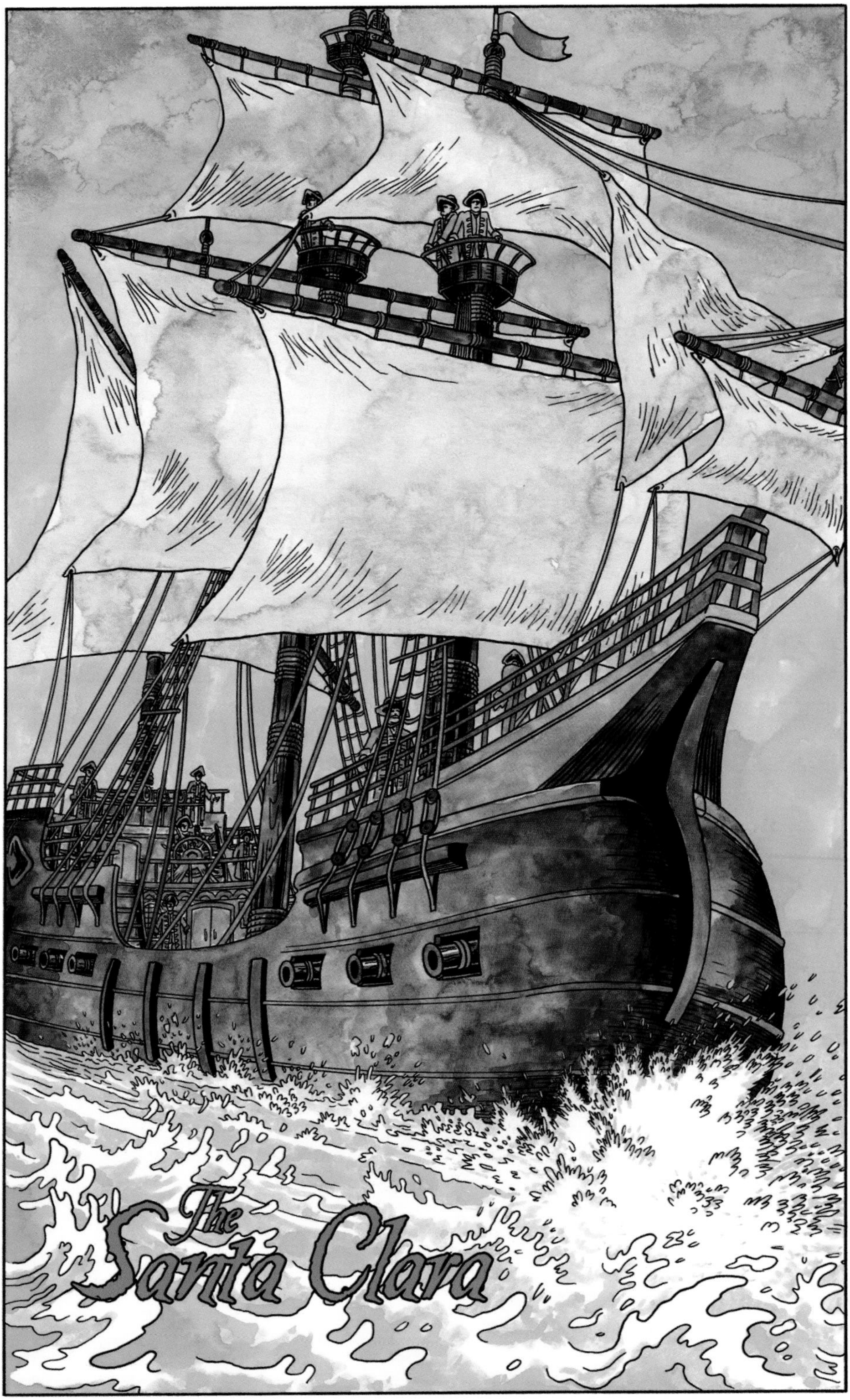
The Santa Clara

75

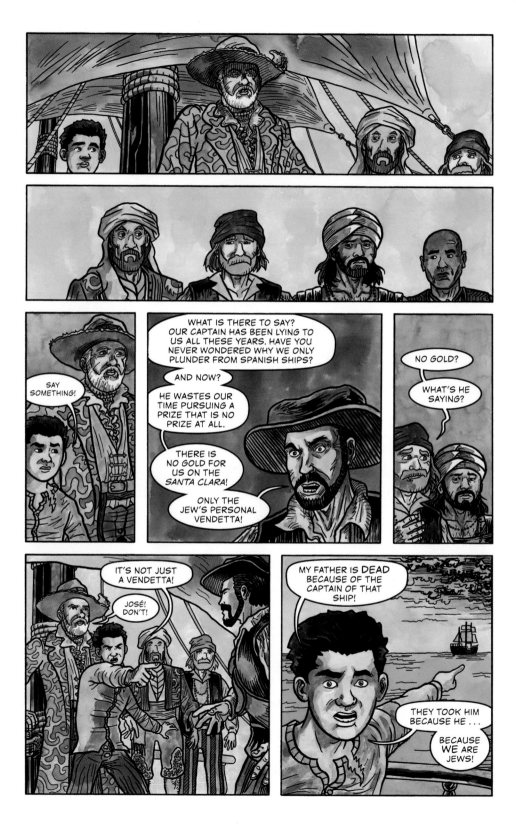

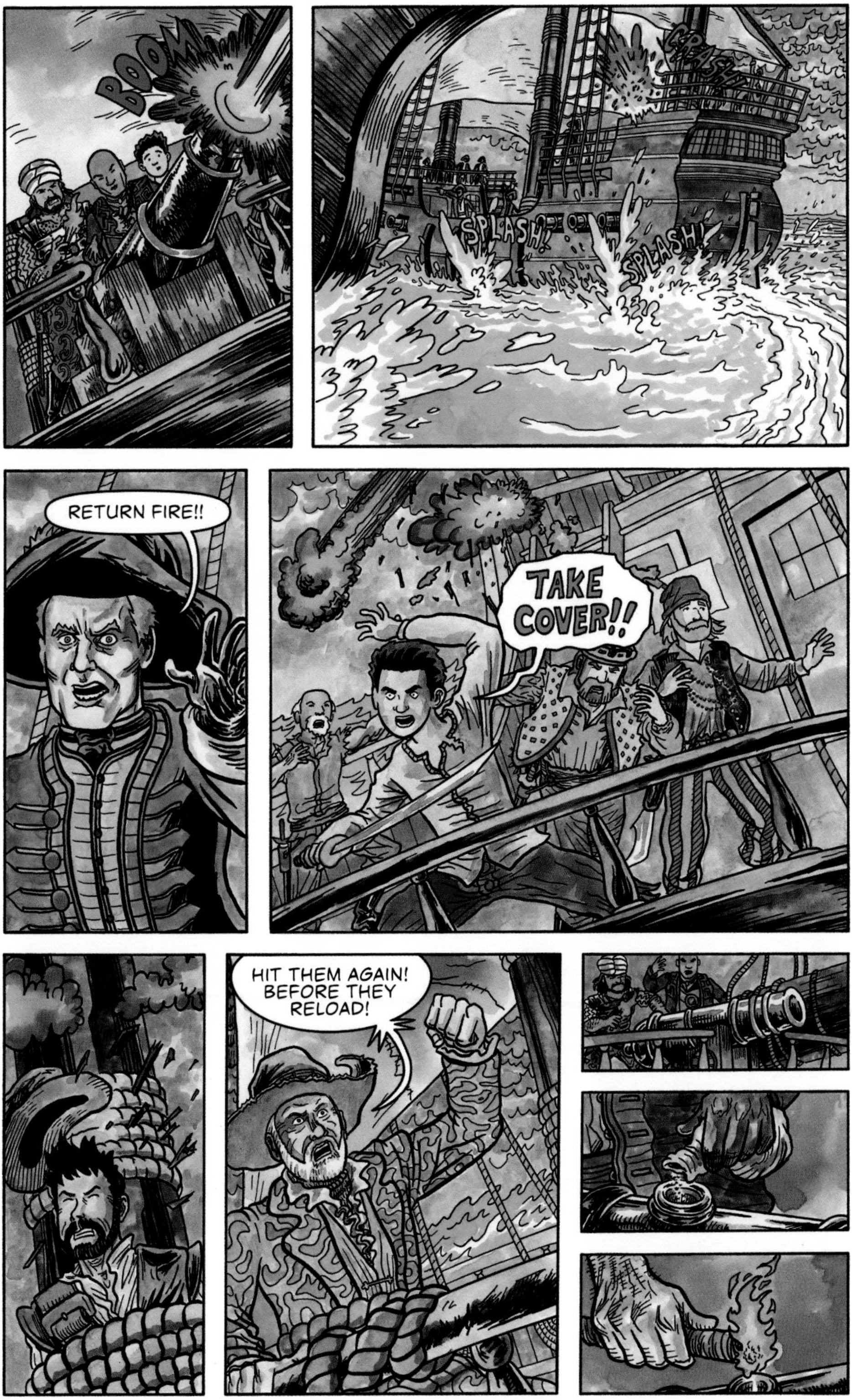
BOOM
CRASH!
SPLASH!
SPLASH!
RETURN FIRE!!
TAKE COVER!!
HIT THEM AGAIN! BEFORE THEY RELOAD!

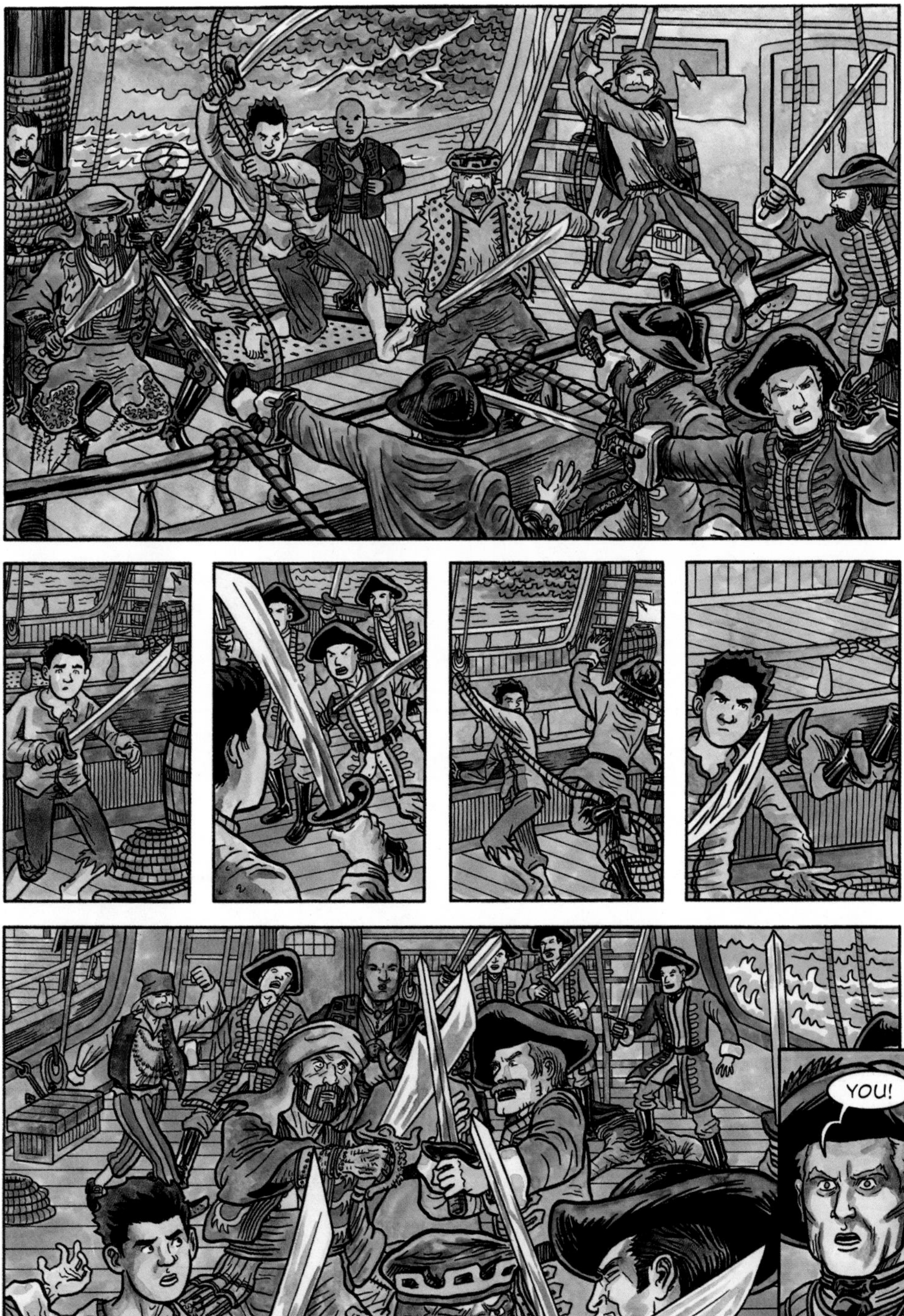
YOU!

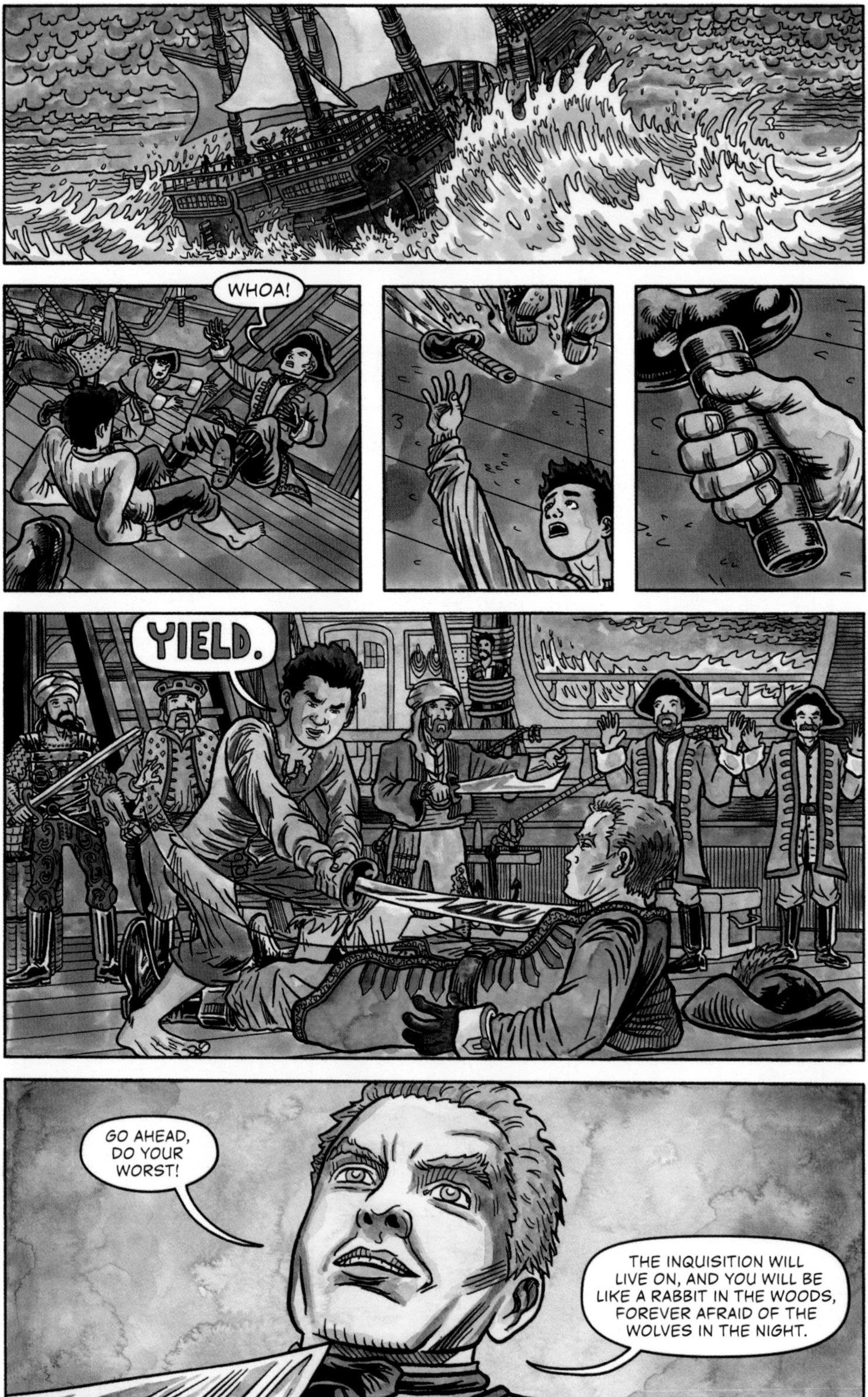
WHOA!
YIELD.
GO AHEAD, DO YOUR WORST!
THE INQUISITION WILL LIVE ON, AND YOU WILL BE LIKE A RABBIT IN THE WOODS, FOREVER AFRAID OF THE WOLVES IN THE NIGHT.

88

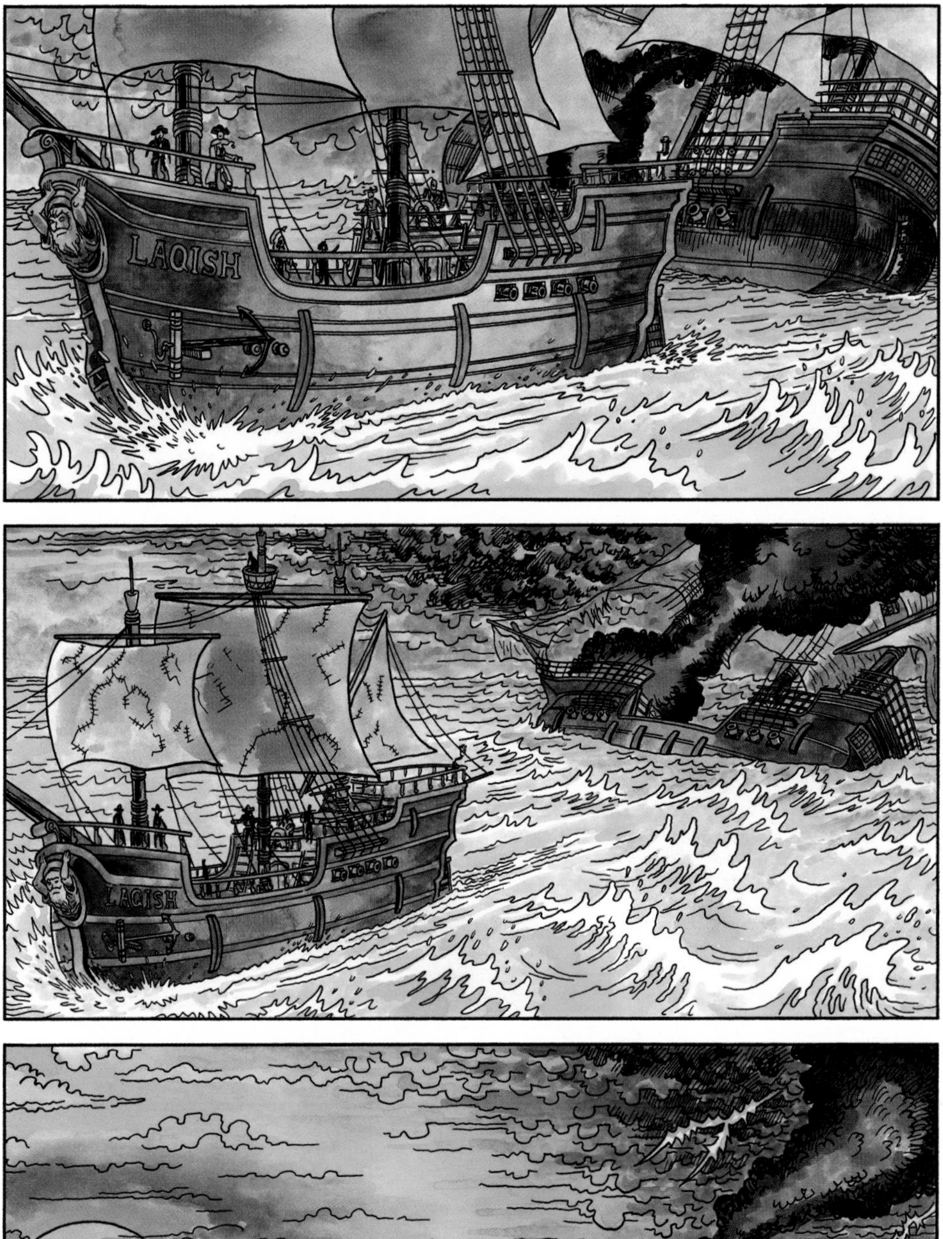
LAQISH
LAQISH
LAQISH

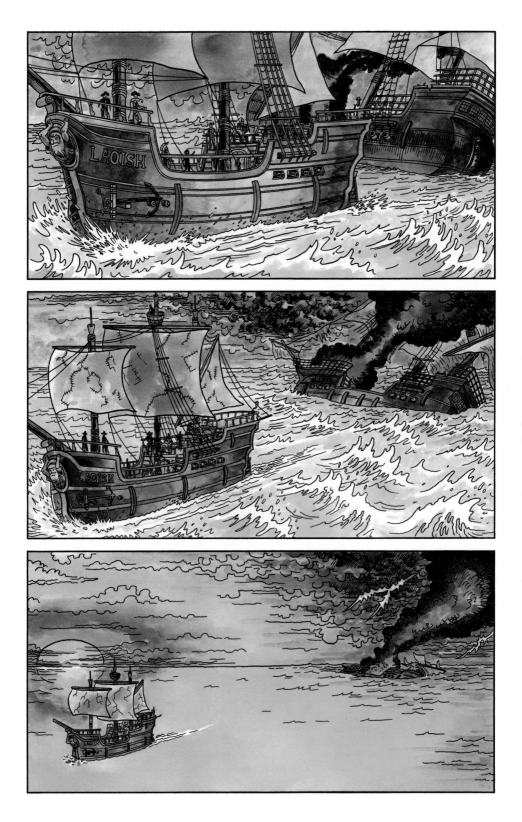

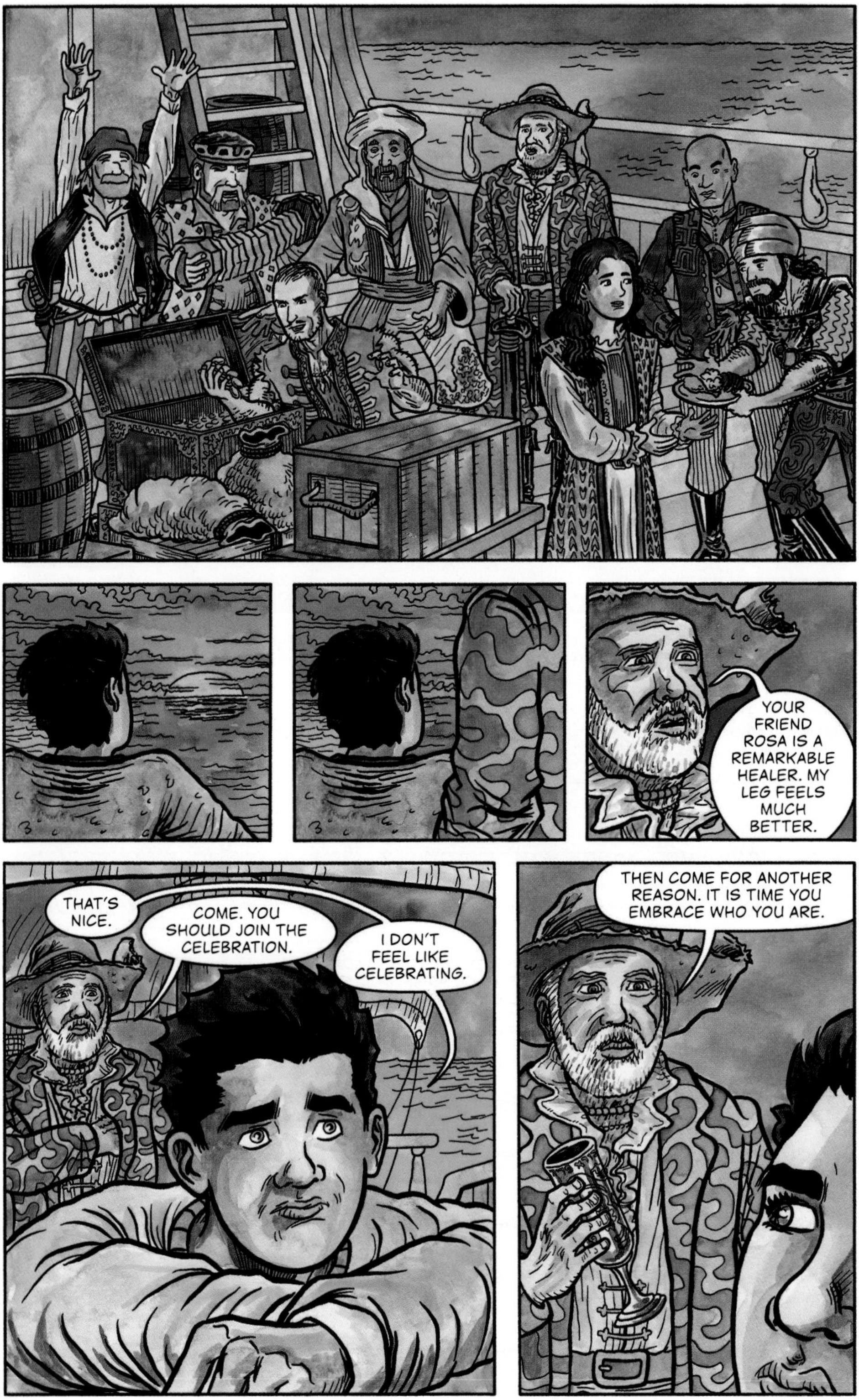
YOUR FRIEND ROSA IS A REMARKABLE HEALER. MY LEG FEELS MUCH BETTER.
THAT'S NICE.
COME. YOU SHOULD JOIN THE CELEBRATION.
I DON'T FEEL LIKE CELEBRATING.
THEN COME FOR ANOTHER REASON. IT IS TIME YOU EMBRACE WHO YOU ARE.

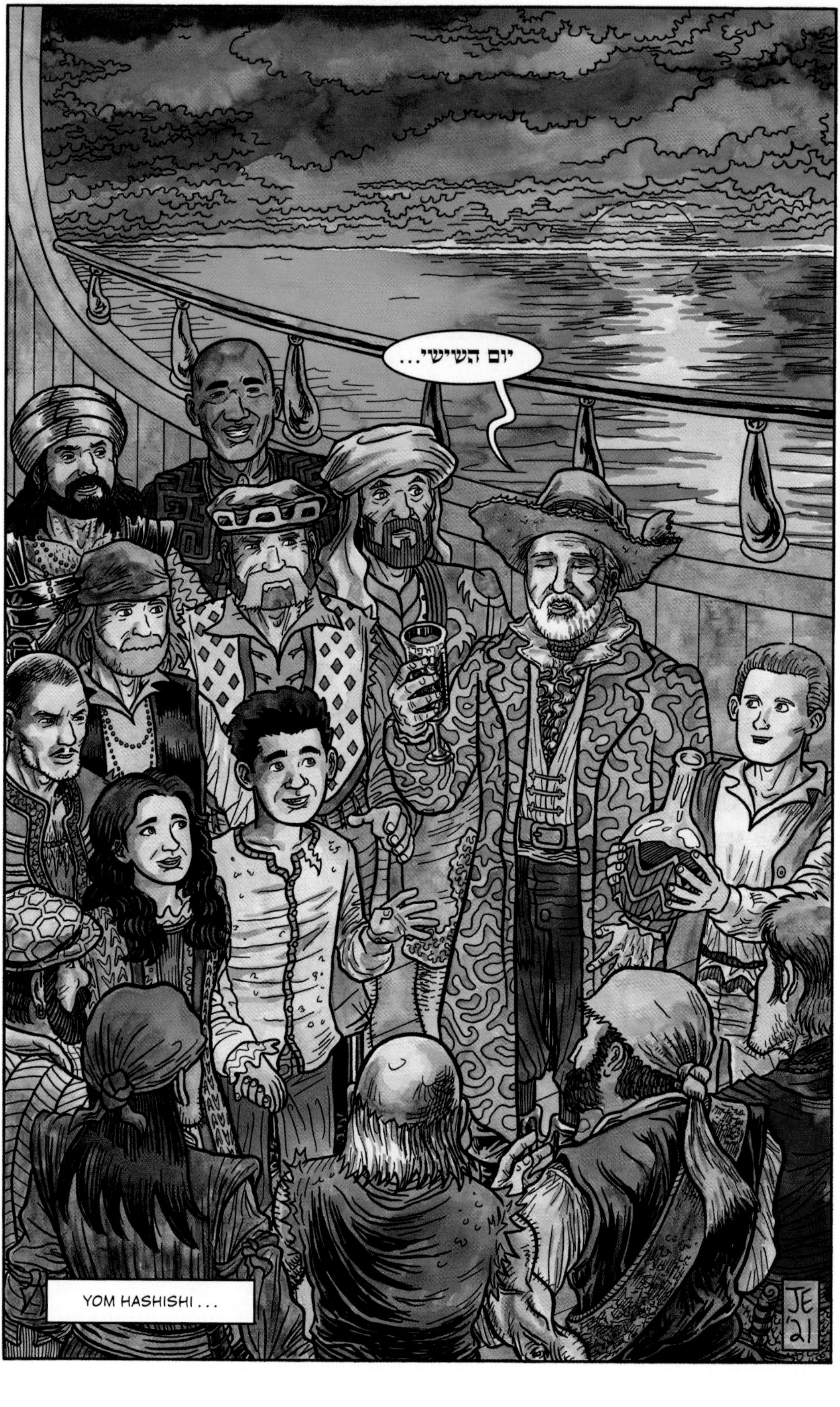
יום השישי...
YOM HASHISHI . . .

Historical Note

In 1492, on the very day of Columbus's departure, the Edict of the Expulsion of the Jews took effect in Spain. It ordered all Jews to leave Spain forever -- or face terrible consequences. Some Spanish Jews escaped to the sea, including members of Columbus's expedition. So, were there really Jewish pirates? Historians debate this question, but you can look up Samuel Palache, Moses Cohen Henriques, Sinan Reis, or Yaacov Kuriel and decide for yourself.

About the Author

Arnon Z. Shorr is a filmmaker and screenwriter. He grew up between worlds: half Sefaradi and half Ashkenazi, a Hebrew speaker living in America, a Jewish private-school kid in a mostly non-Jewish suburb. Whenever he'd set foot in one world, his other foot would betray him as *different*. That's why he tells stories that embrace the peculiar, where things that are different are the keys to survival and success. If you'd like to learn more about Arnon, his book, films, and screenplays, visit www.arnonshorr.com.

About the Illustrator

Joshua M. Edelglass is the assistant director of Camp Ramah New England. His illustrations have appeared in a variety of newspapers and magazines, and he illustrated stories for *The Jewish Comix Anthology*, published by Alternate History Comics. His artwork has appeared in numerous exhibitions, including *Pow! Jewish Comics Art and Influence* (Brooklyn, 2018); *JOMIX -- Jewish Comics: Art and Derivation* (New York & Philadelphia, 2016); and *The Jew as the Other* (New York, 2015). Joshua's writings about movies, television, comic books, and more can be found at www.JoshuaEdelglass.com.

Acknowledgments

We could not have made this book without help, guidance, and support from many people, including (but not limited to) Avigail Appelbaum-Charnov, for historical architecture guidance; Kate Farrell, for pitch notes and support; Joanne Lewis, for notes on Taino history and culture; Richard Rasner, for all things Pirate; and the entire cast and crew of *The Pirate Captain Toledano* for making the film that led to this book. A special tip of the hat to Diana Haberstick (CDG), whose original costume designs for the film inspired some of the clothing illustrations here, and to Stephen DeCordova, who gave Captain Toledano his face and voice. Thank you to our agent, Anna Olswanger, who was first to recognize this book's potential. We also thank Joni Sussman, along with Viet, Danielle, Taylor, and the teams at Kar-Ben and Lerner for being such supportive partners. Josh would like to thank Rabbi Ed Gelb and the entire Camp Ramah New England team, for being so supportive and helping him to find the extra time he needed to complete his work on this book. Josh is also deeply grateful to Steph, Tahlia, and Reya for their love and their understanding of the many, many hours he spent hiding away in the basement, drawing! And Arnon thanks Talia, Adir, Ilana, and Margalit, who let him write in peace (in the walk-in closet) during the first weeks of the COVID lockdown.

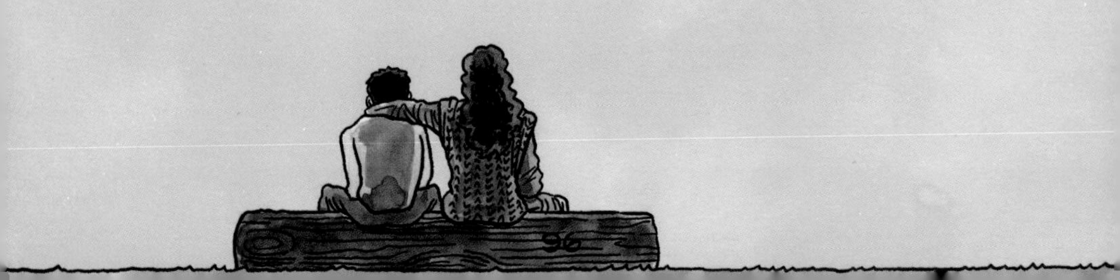